FIGHT FOR WET SPRINGS

CHARLIE STEEL
Tale-Weaver Extraordinaire

FIGHT FOR WET SPRINGS

CHARLIE STEEL
Tale-Weaver Extraordinaire

Condor Publishing, Inc.
Lincoln, Michigan

FIGHT FOR WET SPRINGS
by Charlie Steel

October 2019

Copyright © 2003 by Condor Publishing, Inc

Library of Congress Control Number: 2019950056

First Printed 2003

Second Edition Published 2019

ISBN-13: 978-1-931079-31-0

Condor Publishing, Inc.
PO Box 39
123 S. Barlow Road
Lincoln, MI 48742
www.condorpublishinginc.com

Illustrations by Gail Heath, Harrisville, Michigan

Printed in the United States of America

DEDICATION

This book is dedicated to Frederick Faust (Max Brand) who often took creative flights of fancy to explore and examine the human condition. It is hoped that this Young Adult Western is in that vein and captivates anyone who reads it.

NOTE TO READERS & WRITERS:

In 2003, the first edition of FIGHT FOR WET SPRINGS was newly published and printed in a very limited edition. This is a completely revised second edition

ILLUSTRATIONS

CHAPTER ONE

The hot sun beat down unmercifully and further baked the beige and yellow land. Barren rocks steamed vapors and mirages of heat that from a distance looked like moving pools of dark water. Cottonwood leaves drooped silver-green brightness. Cattle, yellow grass, and rocks spotted the valley where the far side dipped to gray shimmering flatness and then rose up again in an array of pastel colors that extended to the distant purple mountains. The air was dry, the heat sucking moisture out of everything so that the sky was crystal clear and one could see land and mountains a hundred miles away.

A cabin lay nestled in a copse of cottonwoods and pines in the large valley below. A small mountain stream flowed lazily through the grove and past the little home. The sun reflected off its veranda roof that provided shelter to a young mother darning socks at a small table. Every few minutes the woman shaded her eyes with her hand and stared out at the stream. She squinted into the light as the sun pierced through the leaves and glistened off the rushing water. In front of the porch, in a pool created by a small rock formation, splashed a deeply tanned, freckle-faced boy.

"Look at this, Mommy!" The boy sped a toy boat across the crystal water.

"Come out now, Kurt West, before you turn blue or get sunburned."

"Aww, do I have to?"

"Yes, now!"

Kurt splashed his way up out of the pool, taking his boat with him. Water streamed from his cutoff pants as he ran to the porch. He climbed onto a chair next to his mother and shook his hair, flinging water in every direction.

"Kurt! You're getting me and my work all wet," his mother laughed.

"When do we eat, Mommy? I'm hungry."

"It's ready in the kitchen. Suppose you bring it out here. We'll eat on the porch."

The boy jumped down, opened the screen door, and went into the house, leaving a trail of water drops that evaporated as quickly as they hit the warm floor.

"Kurt, don't try to carry it all at once."

The child made several trips carrying stoneware plates of cold roast beef, cheese, and bread. Priscilla West and her son sat in the shade of the porch enjoying their lunch.

A group of riders appeared in the distance, their horses kicking up dust. Priscilla saw them and quickly got up and pushed the boy into the house.

"What is it, Mommy? I'm still hungry."

"Shhh! Be quiet, dear. Some men are coming, and I don't know who they are."

She ran to the fireplace and took down a rifle. It was loaded, but she checked anyway to make certain there was a shell in the Winchester's chamber. The boy and his mother stood and watched for a long time as the men on horses rode closer. There were five riders and, as they rode nearer to the cabin, Priscilla identified the brand as belonging to Poindexter's outfit. She was afraid of that.

"Are they bad men, Mommy?"

"Hush, Kurt. Promise me you won't say a word." She kept her eyes on the visitors.

The men rode into the yard, kicking up a storm of dust. They started to get down as Priscilla stepped out onto the porch, rifle in hand.

"No one offered you hospitality here. And, no one told you to dismount. State your business and be gone." She lifted the rifle menacingly.

The largest of the five men, dressed in black, spoke up, "The name's Carpenter, ma'am. Bill Carpenter, Poindexter's foreman."

"I know who sent you. What do you want?"

"Not very friendly, ma'am. We were sent over here on an errand. Would Mr. West be about?"

"You don't see him, do you?"

"No, ma'am."

"What you got this minute is the boy, me, and this Winchester. State what you want."

"You're not very hospitable, ma'am."

"Should I be, considering all the trouble we have had with your spread and your men? Last year nearly all our calves were branded with your mark. What do you want?"

"Ma'am, the boys here and myself will tell you up front that we had nothing to do with that branding last year.

3

The boss sent me over to sort of palaver like and keep everything friendly."

"Friendly's nice. Just keep sittin' up on those ponies and state your business."

"Have it your way. Poindexter knows you're having trouble with keeping hands, rustling and misbranding and all…"

"And…"

"Well, he authorized me to make a fair offer for your spread. The boss wants you and your husband to think about it. If you agree, he invites you up to his ranch for dinner and to talk it out."

"Tell him for Mr. and Mrs. West that the answer is 'no.' We worked too hard to sell for any price. This place is our boy's legacy."

"Aren't you even going to talk it over with your husband, ma'am?"

"I told you, I'm speaking for him, too. Time's up. Now move along."

The five horsemen sat and watched the lady with the rifle. When Carpenter turned his horse, the others followed. The foreman shouted back over his shoulder. "Mr. Poindexter is dead set on this land, Mrs. West. Maybe you and your husband should reconsider."

"We'll never sell—you hear me? Never!"

The horsemen rode swiftly south—back toward the flat gray valley. The dust trail that marked their passage hung in the dry air long after they were out of sight.

"I didn't say anything, Mommy. Did I do good?

"Yes, Kurt, you were wonderful." Priscilla bent down

and gave her son a big hug.

The mother picked up the dishes and carried them into the house. She kept both the rifle and Kurt close to her the rest of the day. With nervous impatience, she waited for her husband and the hired hands to come home. The afternoon passed, and it grew later and later. Still, no John West, nor any of his three-man crew, returned. She fixed dinner, and she and her son ate alone. It began to get dark.

Priscilla paced back and forth in the small but tidy cabin. She got out paper and pencil and began to write and draw sketches.

"What are you doing, Mommy? Can I draw, too?"

She gave the boy a pencil and paper. "Take your time, Kurt."

Priscilla drew a picture of the cabin with an addition of a flat log roof with a parapet. Next, she added a cellar under the cabin and connected it by a tunnel to a root cellar and a stable.

It was getting dark, and still the men had not returned. She got up and lit a kerosene lamp. Growing increasingly worried, Priscilla went back to her drawing. She figured out a supply list, tried to estimate the cost of the items, finished, and put the pencil down.

"Look at the ranch I drew, Mommy. See the house, the trees, and the horse? That's you, Daddy, and me. And these three are Charlie, Dan, and Shorty. Do you like my picture?"

"Very good, Kurt. See if you can draw another on the back."

The woman got up and began to rummage through

the cabin. She gathered and placed on the kitchen table a Bowie knife, two .38 revolvers, a .36 percussion cap & ball pistol, and boxes of ammunition. Against the wall, she leaned two double-barreled shotguns, one with a broken stock, and two Winchester rifles.

Kurt, seeing what his mother was doing, went into his bedroom and came back with a wooden Bowie knife in a leather scabbard, a wooden pistol, holster, and belt—toys carved for him by the ranch hands and his father. He put his weapons on the table. Priscilla smiled.

"Is this good, Mommy? Why are we doing this?"

"To see if we have everything we need to protect ourselves," his mother answered.

At that moment they heard horses ride up and head to the corral. Priscilla turned down the lantern, picked up a Winchester, and pointed it towards the back door. John West and his three hands came barging in. They were hungry, and food was on their minds. The men stopped abruptly when they saw Priscilla with the rifle in her hands and the pile of weapons on the table.

"Woman! For gosh sake, what's going on here?"

"Don't you shout at me, John West. We had visitors. I'll tell you about it after you eat. Here," she said, putting the Winchester down. "Help me clear off the table."

Her husband started to insist on an immediate explanation but one look at his wife's face, and he decided to do as she asked.

The men removed the weapons from the table. John gathered stoneware dishes and knives and forks from the top of the oak sideboard and placed them around the table.

Priscilla took food from the warming oven. There was a roast, potatoes, gravy, onions, and carrots. The golden crust on a fresh loaf of bread steamed as her knife sawed into it and thick slices were piled on a plate. Next to it, she placed freshly churned butter. An apple pie lay on the stove. The four men sat down and began to eat ravenously. Priscilla glared. They immediately improved their manners.

With the last of the apple pie eaten and another cup of coffee poured for each, the men sat quietly and waited for Priscilla to explain what happened. She picked up the dishes, piled them in the sink in front of the pump, then sat in the end chair at the large kitchen table. For a moment, she blocked out the voices around her and reflected back and remembered what made the ranch what it was today.

She looked at the three hired men. Charlie, Shorty, and Dan had been part of the ranch for more than ten years, ever since Priscilla and John had started it from one section. The hands were the ones who helped make the place profitable, and more than once, they had risked their lives against rustlers. Over the years, other men had come to work for the Wests. Most of them were good workers but quit after being harassed on the range or in town by Poindexter's crew. Charlie, Shorty, and Dan, on the other hand, had endured the intimidation. It was because they were treated fairly by the Wests that they stayed. Priscilla doctored them when they were sick, listened to their problems, and fed them at her table. They knew they had a home for life.

They loved the ranch, too. The place was special

because of its box canyon, large in length and width. At the canyon's beginning, up next to the mountain rock, were the springs that gave the spread its name, Wet Springs. The water ran all year, and this is what made the land so valuable. Because of the rock formations, the place was protected in three directions. These three men made the ranch what it was.

It had been ten years of luck and hard work that brought the Wests such success. The three hands had adopted the young couple when John first returned to the West with his bride. John had met Priscilla during a trip back east to visit his family. It was at his sister's house in Detroit when he first saw her and knew she was the one he wanted as his wife. She was the first strong-willed woman he had ever met. Not only was she lovely, but she had brains. Before she agreed to quit her job as a nursing instructor and marry him, she made it clear that she would have a say-so in all things. It was his promise that won her hand. Priscilla brought her life savings, and together they homesteaded their first section of the range.

The men, still holding their coffee cups, slid their chairs back from the table.

"Perhaps what Mrs. Priscilla has to say is not meant for our ears," said Charlie.

"On the contrary, Charlie," said Priscilla. "I want you to hear what I have to say."

"When don't we ever listen to you, Priscilla?" laughed her husband.

"This is no laughing matter. Poindexter wants our

ranch. He sent five men to scare us. I've been thinking all day about this, and I've come up with some ideas. You may not agree, but I'm intractable."

"Ma'am?" questioned Shorty.

"It means we can't change her mind," answered John.

Priscilla glared at her husband and continued, "I won't be overruled. If you don't agree, I will have no choice but to take Kurt and leave. I won't risk my son."

She had their attention now.

"At noon five riders came from the south. I was prepared with a rifle before they got close. The brand was Poindexter's. The spokesman said his name was Bill Carpenter—foreman, he said."

"I know him, ma'am," said Shorty. "He and I rode together ten years back. Then he was a decent fellow as far as that goes. Looks like Poindexter sent someone with manners."

"Well, they made to light down, and I pointed the rifle. I told them to state their business and be gone. Carpenter said that because of the rustling and other problems we were having, Poindexter would make a fair offer on the ranch."

"Yeah, after he creates trouble, he offers to buy you out," Charlie said, banging his fist on the table.

"I told him, 'no.' In parting, the foreman said that Poindexter wants this land and we better reconsider. I lost my temper and told him we'd never sell."

"I'm sorry you had to face them alone, Priscilla. I should have been here."

"Would you have done anything differently, John?"

"No, I wouldn't. Now, what's this idea you have?"

"You're not going to like it, but hear me out. What I've been thinking is that we're too vulnerable."

"Come on, Priscilla," growled John. "We're practically enclosed on three sides."

"Practically is right. The rocks provide cover from the weather and wind, but do nothing to prevent Poindexter's crew from boxing us in."

"She's right about that, boss," agreed Charlie.

"Will you men stop interrupting?"

Priscilla brought the drawings and the lists. She put them on the table in front of her.

"Poindexter starts out polite by making an offer. At the same time, he has his cowboys whittle away at a rancher's herd. Then the rancher's cowhands are intimidated and threatened, so they quit. Am I right?"

The men nodded.

"No one has stood up to Poindexter. So far the ranchers have given in and left."

"That's a fact," said Shorty.

"So, this is what I propose. We gather all the cattle we can herd up and drive to the railhead. We do it at night and as quickly as possible—then sell at whatever price we can get."

"Priscilla! Are you crazy? We're just now building up the herd. In a few years, we'll be sitting comfortable and can afford to extend the ranch buildings. For years we've planned to buy better bulls, build a dam, and irrigate for grain and better grass. Just what are you thinking of?"

"This, John West. Poindexter won't be satisfied until he

has the ranch. He doesn't care who he kills to get it. I don't want to lose you, but you have to decide for yourself. I will not put Kurt at risk. If you don't do as I ask, I'll take Kurt and leave. What good is one hundred percent of nothing? Sure as the sun rises, Poindexter will eventually come up here to run the cattle off. If he doesn't kill us, what will we live on then? The only way to survive this is to outthink that crook. Every rancher he has gone after, he's beaten, so we might as well sell our cattle for what we can get."

"Never!" thundered her husband. He slammed his hand on the table. "I'm not selling the herd. We came too far to quit now."

"Well, John," said Priscilla giving her husband a determined glare. "You are selling my half of the herd. I'm calling in your vow that I have fifty percent say-so. Half the money I get I will salt away; the other half I'll use to buy supplies and to make the changes I drew on this paper. Here, look at this."

John studied the drawing and the list, then passed them to the other men.

"If we do this, they'll have a hard time burning or shooting us out," she explained. "We need to purchase ammunition, cases of rifles, pistols, and shotguns. We'll lay in surplus food and supplies. We already have water."

"Priscilla, I don't know about this. When I said you had a say-so, I meant when we agreed together."

"John West, you knew when you married me that you got a woman who can think for herself. I see how this is going to turn out. It would be a mistake not to sell all the cattle now. You're going to wake up one morning and the cattle will be gone, and there won't be anything you can do about it. Once you've lost the stock, you will have lost the money those cattle could have earned. Money that could have kept this ranch going far into the future."

"What future, Priscilla? A ranch with no livestock? And, when do we buy cattle and start up again? I won't do it. I won't sell out."

"John, I either get to sell my half of the herd and stock up on supplies or else I leave."

"Hold it, hold it," said Charlie waving both hands in the air. "What you both say makes sense. Now, John, we know the Missus. If she says she has her mind set, then we know what that means. We don't want to see this place split up. Why don't you both do what you think is right? That's not too much of a compromise. John, you go with your plan and, Mrs. Priscilla, you go with yours. What do you think, boys?"

"Well, since you both need our help to carry it through, perhaps we do have a say in this one," replied Shorty. "I'll go with John and help with the herd."

"You know I like to build," said old Dan. "So I'll follow Mrs. West's plan to fort the place up."

"What do you say, John?" asked Charlie.

"Priscilla," said John, "I won't have nothing to do with driving the herd to the rail line, but you can do whatever you want with your half. I'm telling you though, I don't like it, and I'm sleeping in the bunkhouse."

"And don't you come back begging to me, John West, for a little affection and understanding after your half of the herd is rustled. Eventually, you'll see my plan is the right one. I won't even say I told you so."

The four men got up and started for the back door.

"Dan," said Priscilla, "please stay. I'd like to go over these drawings and determine costs. I also want to go over the supply list, and the price of cattle at the railhead."

John, Charlie, and Shorty trooped out of the house. John looked like he had been bitten by a scorpion.

"Can we move the cattle at night," asked Priscilla, "and get to the railhead in secret? And what about buying guns and supplies?"

The three men heard what she said as the door closed.

"Well, I married her," growled John, "for better or worse. But, I sure do hate to lose cattle. Just when we are getting ahead."

"That little lady has brains," said Charlie. "Maybe what she says is peculiar, but it may save the ranch."

"Look at it this way, Boss," said Shorty swiping a sulfur match across the bottom of his boot and lighting a cigarette. "What she said ain't crazy, and you can never have too many supplies. I don't agree with her figuring that Poindexter will come down on us that hard, but I do agree that he will try to make things pretty difficult for Wet Springs. He don't take "no" easily."

The three men walked to the bunkhouse. "Hey!" yelled John as he flopped down on an empty cot. "One of you swell-heads throw me a blanket and a pillow, will yeah?"

CHAPTER TWO

During the day the three ranch hands rounded up cattle. John stayed out of it and performed other chores. Priscilla saddled up and joined the men while Kurt sat in the saddle in front of her. There was a lot of ground to cover and many unbranded calves. There were several Wet Springs cows with calves holding the Poindexter brand. Under Priscilla's instructions, they were rebranded.

Priscilla worried about Poindexter's men and kept a lookout on high ground. If the ruthless rancher got wind of the roundup, she was sure he would stop it. She saw none of his hands, but that didn't mean someone might not be watching.

In five days, they had rounded up six hundred head of combined stock. There were many more cattle to be culled, and most of them were in the boxed canyon to the north of the ranch. The canyon was full of brush, lush green meadows, and sloping ridges. There were cattle in there that were wild and had never been branded.

At night around the kitchen table, Priscilla discussed with her ranch hands what to do. Charlie and Shorty estimated the entire herd to be double what they had already found. Dan recommended leaving the calves and going to market with the remaining herd. Priscilla insisted on taking and selling the calves no matter what price she got for them.

One night at dinner, Priscilla announced she felt they were ready and she wanted to start the drive the next night. Dan was out guarding the herd. After more debate, it was agreed that she and the three hands would drive the cattle to the railhead. They would bypass the town and meet the train farther up. Priscilla said they would let the herd graze by day and move it by night.

John remained petulant and sulked at the dinner table. He still refused to help with the cattle drive, and Priscilla hardly spoke to him. She was all plans and action. John would be left to care for Kurt in her absence.

They finished eating, and Priscilla stacked the dishes. The men were drinking their coffee at the table when she spun around. "Why not go tonight? We're ready. I have a feeling if we wait, it'll be too late."

"You can't be serious," said John. "You can't just up and leave in the middle of the night—especially a night like this. It's brewing for a storm."

Priscilla became more determined, "Luck and surprise are on our side; any time now Poindexter's men might see the gathered herd."

Priscilla went to the corral, saddled her horse, and loaded the five-day supply of food onto two packhorses. They would travel without a wagon and move at night. The sky was beginning to blacken with clouds, and a cool wind was blowing. A steady downpour could hide the herd's tracks.

She went back to the cabin and put on her .36 cap & ball; then she picked up a .44 rifle.

"Get your butts moving!" she ordered as she saw the men still sitting at the table drinking coffee. "I'll go tell Dan we're leaving tonight."

She grinned at the looks she received. She shocked them; she shocked herself. The old Priscilla West had never talked like that. If this world was going to be relentless to her, she had the right to give some of it back. She smiled grimly to herself as she put on a slicker and a wide-brimmed sombrero. The outfit made her look like a man.

"I'll start the herd myself, boys, if you don't get moving."

Kurt came running up to his mother and wrapped his short arms tightly around her legs. She bent down, hugged her young son, and kissed his cheek.

"Be good, Kurt, and mind Daddy. I'll be home soon." She clenched her jaw, went outside, and mounted her horse.

The men and the boy followed her onto the porch.

"Take good care of him," she told her husband. "Near as I figure, we'll be back in eleven days."

John swallowed hard as he watched his stubborn wife grab the packhorse's reins, slap her horse, and ride east toward the herd. Charlie and Shorty followed, riding out of the corral. A flash of lightning lit the sky and silhouetted the figures. Kurt held his father's leg and in a trembling voice called out, "Bye, Mommy."

After the riders were completely out of sight, John closed the cabin door and took Kurt to his bedroom behind the kitchen and helped him into his flannel nightshirt. Neither father nor son felt like stories tonight. John hugged Kurt, holding him a bit longer than usual, and tossed him playfully into bed. They both forced a laugh, and John tucked the covers under the boy's chin.

John walked into the bedroom that he had shared with Priscilla these many years. For the first time since their marriage, he was alone and away from his wife. Feelings of love, pain, and remorse ate at him. He should be on that trail drive—not his wife. Still, it was agreed that from now on, until Poindexter was out of the picture, that no one would be left alone. He couldn't say that Priscilla, riding with the three trusted ranch hands, was unprotected. With that thought for solace, John took a pistol and a rifle into the bedroom. That was something else that Priscilla had insisted on. John undressed and slid between the sheets and under the covers. He could smell the sweet scent of his wife. John lay there staring into the dark for a long time before falling into a fitful sleep.

Dawn finally came. John got up, dressed, and began to fix breakfast. When the food was ready, he went to Kurt's bedroom door. "Wake up, sleepyhead," he called. "Are you going to stay in bed all day?" Kurt jumped to the floor with a giggle. Together they had oatmeal, toast, and coffee.

John opened the back door, breathed deeply, and smelled the fresh, clean air that followed the night's rain. He stepped off the veranda and headed to the outhouse behind the cabin. While sitting there, he began to hear the bawling of cattle, and his nerves went tight. There he sat with his pants down, no pistol or rifle in hand. It was evident that someone was moving and disturbing the herd. John pulled up his trousers and ran for the house.

Once inside, he took a pair of field glasses and scoped the land behind the cabin. All he could see were areas of movement too far away to identify. There was no dust because of the rainstorm. Something was moving out there, and it appeared to be at the mouth of the canyon. Ordinarily, he would have saddled a horse, ridden over, and checked it out. He was alone now, no—worse—he was with Kurt. And his first responsibility was the safety of his son.

"What's going on, Daddy?"

"Someone or something is moving the last of our cattle, Son."

"Are they rustlers? Can we get on our horses and chase them away?"

"I wish it was that easy, Kurt. There are not enough of us to take on anyone."

"Daddy, you take your rifle, and I'll take mine. We'll get em'."

John smiled. "No, we'll play it safe and stay right here with our guns ready."

By the middle of the day, it was evident that Wet Springs was being rustled of its remaining stock. Through the field glasses, John could see groups of riders hazing cattle from the mouth of the canyon and herding them for a drive. John sat there, unsure of what to do. He couldn't put his son at risk. Everything Priscilla had said came back to him. If it weren't for her quick and determined action, they would have nothing left. The rainstorm must have obliterated the tracks of the other herd; otherwise, they would have been chased down by this group of riders. The storm had protected them.

"Kurt, I want you to stay inside the cabin. I'm going out there on foot and have a look at those rustlers."

"You don't want my help, Daddy?"

"I want you to stay and guard the cabin. Can you do that?"

"Okay, Daddy."

If Priscilla found out what he was doing, she would have his head. *I can't just stand by and do nothing*, he thought.

John kept to low ground, and after a long walk, he made it into rifle range. There appeared to be five to six hundred cattle already herded up. John could see five cowboys guarding them. From the canyon came more bawling of cattle and what looked like ten more riders pushing a group of a hundred more cattle out onto the rolling meadow. It seemed like this was the end of their hurried roundup.

John waited until the last of the cattle and riders met with the main herd. Against better judgment, but in anger, he took aim with his rifle and began to shoot. He knocked two cowboys out of the saddle before the riders and cattle began to scatter.

As John worked his way back to the cabin, a rustler on higher ground spotted him and began shooting. John ran as fast as he could and jumped into a small gully. He turned, aimed, and shot the rustler.

Others were working their way to flanking positions, and a fusillade of shots began striking the dirt around him.

Again he ran for the cabin attempting to keep to cover. Near the house, John came out of a depression, and there was another barrage of shots. He was hit and fell.

Perched on a box, Kurt watched from the cabin window and saw his father fall. The boy saw armed strangers on foot and others on horses come forward. Kurt jumped down, ignored the rule about touching a weapon, and grabbed a heavy pistol from a holster and belt hanging over a chair.

Kurt climbed up to the kitchen sink, opened the window above it, and saw the rustlers coming forward. His father lay still on the path to the cabin. With both small hands around the pistol handle, the boy awkwardly cocked, aimed, and fired. The unexpected recoil made the heavy revolver fly out of his hands to clatter in the sink. Kurt picked it up again and cocked it. Holding on more firmly, he fired at the men coming toward his father. Men on horses and foot stopped and shot back at the house. Kurt ignored the flying glass and wood splinters. He kept cocking and firing the pistol. They weren't going to get his daddy. The rustlers, faced with gunfire from the house, backed off and returned to the herd.

Young Kurt defends his injured father.

Kurt waited until the riders reached the cattle before he put down the empty pistol and ran outside to his father. When he got to him, he saw blood welling from a hole in his father's leg and another on his right shoulder. There was a shallow furrow in the top of his father's head, but this one had stopped bleeding.

"Daddy, Daddy?"

When his father didn't answer, Kurt was really afraid for the first time in his young life. He ran into the house, got a cup of water, and returned. He attempted to make his father drink but no success. Kurt threw the water in his father's face. No reaction. He looked at the two wounds oozing blood and ran back in the house for towels. The boy jammed the thick cloth into the wounds on the leg and shoulder, but the bleeding did not stop. The boy took off his belt. He fastened one towel tightly around his father's leg and pulled the belt tight, as he had seen his mother do when Dan had cut his leg while chopping firewood. The bleeding seemed to lessen. Kurt tried to stop the flow of blood in his father's shoulder. Nothing worked.

In desperation, Kurt ran into the house and came back with the flour box. He knew flour got like paste; maybe it would stop the bleeding. Kurt poured the white powder into the top wound and with great difficulty managed to jam handfuls on the back exit wound. Then Kurt applied towels and tied them down. The bleeding slowed and then stopped.

John West lay ten feet from the porch steps, unprotected except by his five-year-old son. Kurt ran back into the house and got blankets. Using one as a pillow for his father's head, the child covered him with the other. Kurt drew a bucket of water from the pump and brought it out. The boy wet a cloth, as his mother had done when he had a fever, and put it on his father's hot forehead. Every half hour or so, Kurt wet his father's lips and attempted to get water into his mouth. This went on the rest of that night, the next day, and on into the following evening before John awoke. The boy slept fitfully next to his father, the pistol reloaded and next to him. The child became more exhausted and afraid. His father had groaned and talked in feverish delirium through the night. This was a lot for a small boy to take. When John opened his eyes, Kurt was nearly overcome with joy and relief.

"Oh, Daddy, I was so scared. Are you all right?"

"Where—where am I?"

"By the back porch. You were shot. I think I got the blood stopped."

"You did that, Son?"

"Yes, Daddy, and I shot at the bad guys, too. Don't be mad, Daddy, they were coming to get you."

"What did you use, your wooden pistol?"

"Oh no, Daddy, your pistol. This one I'm holding. See? I reloaded it, just like you do, with shells from your belt. I've been protecting you while you've been asleep."

John stared at his son and at the pistol in his small hands. He couldn't say anything; he knew Kurt was telling the truth. John looked down at his leg and saw his son's belt and a towel wrapped around it. He painfully touched his right shoulder with his left hand and felt the cloth and looked at the bit of flour on his hands. His boy must have done that, too.

"Son," said John in amazement, "I think you saved my life."

"Can I help you get back in the house, Daddy? I don't know how to cook for you. Mommy never taught me that yet."

Despite the pain, John laughed. "Okay, son, try to help me up."

CHAPTER THREE

In eight days Charlie and Shorty returned to the ranch on a wagon filled with provisions, horses tied behind. They discovered their boss, wounded, lying on the couch in the living room. Kurt, with new authority and maturity, was cooking. The evidence of his father's care before them. A six-gun lay on the table. After the evening meal, Kurt confidently unloaded, cleaned, and oiled the weapon. This astonished the two hands more than anything else.

John told them the story of the rustlers, how he was shot, and how Kurt had scared them off. With pride, the father related how his son had done the doctoring, cooking, cleaning, and nursing. Charlie and Shorty praised Kurt and thumped him on the back.

John finally asked, "Where's my wife?"

"She's alright boss," replied Shorty. "Don't worry, she went on to Dodge and is returning with money and supplies."

While young Kurt was cleaning the big six-shooter, Charlie related how the trail drive went. "The first night it rained so hard we thought we'd drown. At the start of the storm, there was some thunder—that sure helped get the cattle movin'. Then it just rained hard on and off the rest of the night. We were soakin' wet in our slickers and miserable wet on the saddle. Mrs. Priscilla was untiring. She was like two cowboys in one and insisted we push the cattle all night and into the day."

"Sounds just like Priscilla," grumbled John.

"We tried to make a dry camp, but everything was wet," continued Charlie, ignoring his boss. "We managed breakfast and coffee. There was no way we were going to put bedrolls down in the mud, so we packed up and slowly moved the cattle along. By mid-afternoon, things were dried out enough that we could stop and rest. We slept with one of us keeping watch. By dark, we were up and at it again for the rest of the night."

"You could tell that the missus was stiff and sore, but she kept us going," added Shorty. "She sure didn't baby herself none."

"You betcha she didn't," Charlie added. "She made sure we pushed ahead and took advantage of the rain wiping out the herd's tracks. She was everywhere—up front, behind, and standing watch; she never slept. But, boss, we watched over her no matter what she said for us to do. It was like that for the next three nights—only no rain."

John nodded, "I appreciate that. She's one stubborn lady."

"On the morning of the fifth day, we made it to the stockyards. We ran into all kinds of trouble with the railroad. Since the cattle were out season, they wanted to know who the buyers were. That sure stumped us for a while." Charlie shook his head. "We weren't certain how to get around that one."

"But it didn't stump Mrs. Priscilla," grinned Shorty, remembering the lady's determination.

"No, sir, it didn't," agreed Charlie. "Mrs. West started asking questions and sending telegrams. She figured she could find a buyer and get a better price in Wichita. She had the confidence to tell the railroad to send the bill to Dodge City in care of the Palace Hotel, and she'd pay it."

"That's right," said Shorty. "She didn't let nothin stop her."

Charlie continued, "Then, a day later we shoved the cattle on the cars and took count. We had three-hundred-eighty-five head. We lost only fifteen on those night drives.

"At the next town, she had Shorty and me pile off with our horses and go to the largest mercantile. Mrs. West and Dan continued on to Dodge City with the cattle."

"She gave me four hundred dollars, boss, and told me to give it to the store for half the bill if they refused to extend credit. Well, she was right. They took the order but refused to fill it without some proof of payment. I gave them the money, and the owner of the store sent his clerk off for the wagon, and there it is." He pointed to the front of the cabin. "It's right there all filled up with supplies. And so help me, God, that's the whole story, boss."

"Well, if that's the entire story, then my wife should be here!" demanded John.

"Don't worry, boss," said Shorty, lighting a cigarette. "She'll show up before you know it with more wagons, Dan, and the money."

Charlie and Shorty got up wearily and headed toward

the door to go outside to unload.

"I'm going to help, too," said Kurt, beating the men to the door.

"We sure were counting on that," said Charlie patting the boy on the back.

They returned with sacks and boxes. There were canned goods, hundred-pound bags of flour, sugar, oats, rice, and corn.

Shorty, Charlie, and Kurt made trip after trip from the wagon to the house. They brought in extra saddles, harness's, pistols, rifles, and boxes of ammunition. There was so much that they began to stack it in one corner of the living room and then in one of the bedrooms.

"That's all of it for now, boss."

"You say my wife is coming back with two more wagon loads of this stuff?"

"That's right," laughed Shorty. "She believes in being prepared."

The next few days the men stayed close to the ranch. Charlie and Shorty worked on adding a storage area onto the bunkhouse for supplies. John began to feel better and was able to stand and hobble around with a homemade crutch. Kurt tried to help Charlie and Shorty with their carpentry. The four waited and worried for the lady of the ranch.

After dark, on the night of the sixteenth day, the residents of Wet Springs heard a crunching and rumbling of wheels. John jumped up out of bed and, forgetting his wounds and his crutch, limped and hobbled out the back door into the night. He saw, by the light of the moon, two wagons approaching. On the first wagon sat a lady all dressed up in a white dress and carrying a parasol. On her head was a large flowery hat with ribbons and her hair was piled up underneath. Her foot was perched solidly on the wagon's brake while her white-gloved hands held the reins firmly. John stood there and stared. The woman pulled the wagon up to the veranda of the ranch house and stopped.

"Good evening, sir," she said. "Aren't you going to help a lady down?"

"Priscilla? Priscilla West, is that you?"

"It certainly is, John. Are you going to just stand there gawking or will you help me down?"

Kurt, Charlie, Shorty, and then Dan stood in a semicircle on the other side of the wagon and smiled at the jest Priscilla was playing on her husband.

John reached up his arm in an attempt to help Priscilla. He had no strength and, when she leaned on him to step down, he collapsed to the ground. She lost her balance and fell on top of him.

"Ohhh," groaned John.

"John West, what's the matter with you? You spoiled my dress! You spoiled my surprise! You did that on purpose!"

John continued to groan while Charlie and Shorty ran to help her up.

"Mommy," said Kurt. "It's not Daddy's fault. He's been shot."

Priscilla instantly changed her demeanor. "John, are you all right? Tell me, are you okay?"

She knelt down and gently stroked her husband's face. Charlie and Shorty carried him, still moaning, into the house and laid him on the cowhide couch. They turned up the lanterns so Priscilla could see as she removed the bandages and examined the wounds. They were clean and healing. There was nothing for her to do but to change the dressings. Even the wound on John's scalp was scabbed over.

"It looks like you had trouble," said Priscilla. "Mind telling me what happened?"

"I'll tell you, Mommy!" Kurt said excitedly.

Priscilla's mouth opened, and her eyes widened incredulously as Kurt told about shooting at the men who had wounded his father. John nodded, confirming what his son was saying.

"I leave here with my husband in charge and return to find it's my son who keeps him safe."

Kurt beamed from this statement while his mother tightly hugged him and kissed his cheek. John groaned.

There was much chatter and humor across the kitchen table over the next few hours. Kurt asked Charlie to help him fix something to eat, but Priscilla stepped in. "Get out of my kitchen, and maybe I'll feed you."

"I'm mighty grateful to lose that job; that's for sure," said Charlie.

To the astonishment of John and the others, Priscilla stepped out of the elaborate white dress and revealed the pants and red plaid shirt that she was wearing underneath. She gently took off the ribboned hat and placed it on a hook over the fireplace.

"Now I recognize my beautiful wife," teased John. "I was beginning to worry some stranger might have traded places."

Priscilla laughed and then she worked to feed her hungry men. Ignoring the late hour, they went on talking.

They slept until dawn then began unpacking the two wagons. Most of the supplies went into the new storage area attached to the bunkhouse. It was at breakfast that Priscilla sat down and went back over the story of her last days of the trip.

"We were tired by the time we got to the stockyards. It's amazing how few head we lost. Here's the money belt; I'm wearing it. According to my figure book, we got $9,011.00. The rest went for the three wagons and supplies.

"The fellows who sold me the merchandise were sore as blazes at me. They said we had a bad reputation in our neck of the woods, and that we were considered no less than rustlers. Did I ever give them a piece of my mind. I told them what Poindexter really was. Didn't faze the men one bit. But I'm afraid we were overcharged for nearly everything we purchased. At least I think we got what we need to stand off Poindexter."

"Sounds like I couldn't have done better myself," said John.

Priscilla continued. "I stayed in town for an hour and managed to purchase a crate of piglets and a thoroughbred horse. Dan put the pigs in the small barn and the horse in the corral.

"On the way out of town, I nearly ran over a sickly little cat; I brought her along, too. I think we were lucky making it back."

"She's a spunky lady, John," said Dan straight-faced. "She didn't back down from the railroad telegrapher, the buyers in Dodge, or the owners of the mercantile."

"Okay. So, I was wrong, Priscilla, and you were right. But, I got to say you were darn lucky. What do we do now, I mean now that we don't have any cattle?"

"Cheer up, John," said Priscilla. "You said, yourself, the rustlers didn't get all the stock. Find what's left up in the canyon, brand them, and fence it off. The important thing now is we have money to pay taxes, and you have time to work on the ranch and finish our plans."

"What about the thoroughbred horse, Mommy? Are we going to breed foals?"

"Yes, Kurt, I almost forgot. That's something else we can start."

"Can I have the cat, Mommy? She already slept on my bed last night."

"Yes, she's yours. What are you going to call her?"

"I thought about Tiger. That's the way she's striped."

"Tiger's a great name. What do you think, boys?"

CHAPTER FOUR

Weeks passed on Wet Springs Ranch. Armed at all times, the men began work on several small dams in the canyon to provide more water for the cattle and irrigation for better grass. Despite the shortage of cattle, they had enough work to keep them busy for years.

The three hands and John searched the brush in the large canyon and slowly gathered a herd of wild cows, many with calves. It was slow, dangerous, and exhausting work. They discussed Priscilla's idea of building a fence across the mouth of the canyon and decided it would work. Part of the fence would be made of rock. They would simply use dynamite and blow a large section of cliff over. The rest would be made of sturdy cedar poles with a gate.

Priscilla finally broke down and went into the town of Red Wing for the first time in months. It was greatly changed. Many of the stores where she usually did business were now being run by strangers. She tried to do some shopping and was turned away. It was evident that Poindexter's grip was tightening. He owned and controlled more and more of the town. At a restaurant, Priscilla met with the owner's wife, her old friend, Mary Schmidt. Priscilla was taken to the Schmidt's home in the back. Mary quietly informed her of the latest gossip. The news was not good. Priscilla hugged her friend, thanked her for the information, and left.

She then went to visit the Episcopalian minister. Climbing the steps and entering the large wood-framed church, Priscilla allowed her eyes to adjust to the shadows. Rev. Pellett was standing by his office door.

"Good morning, Priscilla. How may I be of service?" The minister did not sound sincere.

"Rev. Pellett, I just heard some very disconcerting information. Lies are being told about us, and I think you can explain what is going on."

The man frowned and remained reticent.

"Preacher, don't play games with me. You know darn well that we are law-abiding citizens. When that illness broke out in town, wasn't I here to help? How dare anyone accuse us of being less than honorable! You know who the reprobate in this matter is. It's Poindexter. So answer me, what are you going to do about it?"

The minister blinked at Priscilla's hard words. "What do you expect me to do?"

"You can defend us in a sermon—you have influence with the congregation. If you won't stand up for honest people against Poindexter, who will? It's getting serious, Reverend. We could be killed if this continues. I bet you don't know half the story of how our cattle were rustled. How my husband was shot, how Poindexter is telling lies—keeping us from purchasing groceries and supplies. And why? Because he wants our land."

"I'm sure it's not all that bad."

"Oh, no, he's got you, too, hasn't he?"

"I have an obligation to the survival of the church, Priscilla. Mr. Poindexter contributes quite generously and has immense social and economic influence."

"You call yourself a man of God? You have a responsibility. If you don't stop him, who will?"

"I'm sorry you feel that way, Mrs. West."

"Oh, now it's Mrs. West. Well, Mr. Pellett, you can go to Hades. Lord pity us all if Poindexter can get control of the church too."

Priscilla stomped out. She was wearing one of her new dresses. She should have come to town in pants and wearing a six-gun instead of holding a silly parasol. At least she would have fit the part of a rustler's wife.

She walked toward the Mexican section of town where most of the buildings were adobe. Children were playing in the street and women were washing their clothes at the village well. Priscilla's destination was the Catholic church, its bell spire and roof stood high over every object in town.

She walked up the wide steps and reached for the iron handle on one of the massive wooden doors. Some kind of counterweight made it open easily. Inside it was cool and dark. The ceiling was high and gave a feeling of vast space. Stained glass windows depicted scenes from the Bible. Over the altar hung a crucifix. Below and to the right was a statue of Mary, beside it were flickering prayer candles. Several elderly ladies were seated in the pews, their heads covered. Smells of incense made the church seem mystical.

She saw a priest in a black robe standing at the front of the church. Noting the women had their heads covered, Priscilla opened her purse, moved aside a small pistol. She took out a kerchief and placed it on her head. The priest saw her hesitation and motioned for her to come forward.

"Is there something you wish, señora?" he asked quietly.

"I hope so. May we speak somewhere privately?"

The priest took her arm and guided her to a secluded alcove at the rear of the church.

"What is it I can do for you?"

"Father, you should know, I'm not Catholic. I am Priscilla West; we have a ranch twenty miles from here in the high country. We are having difficulties with a man called Poindexter."

"Mrs. West, I know your story."

"Yes, but do you know what has happened to us?"

"No. But I do know that when the sickness came, and some of my people went to you, you nursed everyone alike—you did not worry about race or belief or who was wealthy or poor. I know that you are a good and honest person. Is that enough?"

"Thank you. This is why I have come. We are at great risk, and I don't know who else to turn to. We need workers—ones who are willing to help us build defenses against Poindexter's attacks. Do you know of two reliable men willing to live and work at our ranch?"

"Yes, señora, I know of several good men."

"Before you say yes, let me explain the danger. My husband was shot three times when Poindexter's cowboys stole our cattle. We are expecting more trouble any day now."

"I will tell the men and their families. I think they will come anyway. They need the work and the money. They are good builders, hardworking, and honest. You will see."

"When can we expect them?"

"In a few days they will come with all they need to begin work."

"Thank you, Father."

"No! Thank you, Señora West, for thinking of us. Come, I will walk you out."

CHAPTER FIVE

In four days two men, each leading donkeys, walked into the yard at Wet Springs. On the donkeys' backs were tools and stacks of wooden clay molds. The three cowboys, along with Kurt, John, and Priscilla, were there to meet them. Any unusual activity around the ranch was a moment of interest and not to be missed by anyone if it could be helped.

"Father Torres sent us to work for you. I am Carlos Raymondo Jose Escalante, and this is my amigo, Juan Gabriele Mondo Gonzales."

"Welcome to Wet Springs," said John, reaching out to shake hands. "We have been looking forward to your arrival. I am John West, this is my wife Priscilla, our son Kurt, and our hands Dan, Charlie, and Shorty."

Carlos turned to Juan and spoke to him in Spanish. Juan smiled and accepting John's hand said, "Buenos días."

"My friend is a very good craftsman, but he does not speak English," explained Carlos.

The three cowboys smiled and shook hands. "Buenos dias," said Dan.

"Please," said Priscilla, "After you unload the burros,

come back to the house for lunch. We'll talk of the construction and look at the plans."

The newcomers were hesitant to enter the home of their employers but, wishing to give no offense, they complied. The two workmen were seated in chairs next to John. Priscilla would sit as soon as the food was on the table. Kurt, Charlie, Shorty, and Dan joined them.

"Please," said Priscilla, "I will never remember your full names. What can we call you for short?"

"Call me Carlos," replied the one who spoke English. "And this is Juan."

At the end of dinner, they cleared the table. Priscilla showed them the drawings of her plans to change the house, add a root cellar, dig tunnels, and construct a large barn.

Carlos told them that he understood why they would want tunnels. In fact, he had helped build escape routes under the church for the same reasons. In the Mexican community, the Wests plight was well-known. Also, that Señora West had helped their people at the time of the fever. Señor Poindexter was a bad man, and they would be glad to help.

They sat around the table drinking coffee. The donkeys began braying loudly.

They laughed and as a group tramped outside. Priscilla asked Carlos if her plans were possible. Carlos nodded, "All we need is clay, Señora. Lots of clay—and near water if possible. And, as much help as you can give us making adobe bricks."

Priscilla told Carlos and Juan to explain what they

needed, and she would do her best to comply.

John knew an abundance of clay could be mixed on the bank of the stream further down from the cabin where the water began to disappear into dry ground. Taking picks and shovels to this area, they began to dig into the hard clay. They made a deep hole and then Carlos and Juan dug a trench from the little stream. Water poured into the hole. Juan, Carlos, Kurt, and Dan began mixing the clay with their legs and bare feet. It was muddy, greasy, and sticky work that quickly tired out the four of them. Priscilla went back to the cabin and put on a pair of old pants. She returned, took off her boots, and began to tramp in the mud. Not to be outdone, Charlie, Shorty, and John joined her. One by one, they began to realize how absurd they looked. Priscilla playfully gave her husband a shove—he fell and came up covered with mud. He tried to do the same to her and fell once again. Priscilla escaped from the pit.

The Wests washed off the mud and returned to see what they needed to do next. In the hot sun, their wet clothes dried very quickly.

Juan took a long flat board, put it over four large rocks, and made a waist-high table. He went to the pit, filled a bucket with wet clay, and carried it back. Placing a small board under the mold, he poured clay into the wooden form. He ran a leveling tool back and forth over the top and threw aside the excess. He then picked up the board with the mold and carried it to flat ground. Expertly, he laid the board down and slid it and the form away. He left the wet brick to dry in the sun.

"This is how we do it, señora and señor," said Carlos

pointing with his finger. "It would go much faster if we had more molds and more workers."

The rest of the day was spent making molds. It was hot, exhausting work.

At suppertime, Priscilla called the men in to eat. Juan and Carlos were still uncomfortable eating in the home with their employers.

"Señora West," said Carlos hesitantly. "If you do not think it too bold, I have a suggestion. Because of Señor Poindexter, many of my people are out of work. For just a few dollars more, you could hire many and get the job done quicker. As it is, it may take half a year or more."

"Good idea, Carlos. What do you think, John?"

"Sounds good to me."

"Okay, Carlos, bring more workmen, but let's say, not more than ten? Also, you must assure me these workers will not tell anyone what we are doing here."

"Señora West, you need not worry about us talking to Poindexter's men. They hate our people, and we do not like them. Oh, señora, if you please, I have one other suggestion. I see how you cook for all of us, and that is..."

"You don't like my cooking, Carlos?"

"Please Señora West, no wish to offend. I was thinking that cooking for so many men would be a hardship on you and it would be great work. I would like to suggest that Juan and I bring our wives to stay with us here and they can do the cooking for all of us. This, too, would not be a great expense to you but would be less work."

Priscilla looked to the others who nodded their heads.

"Yes, Carlos, bring your wives. I would appreciate their help."

"Yippee!" yelled Kurt. "Now I get to eat Mexican food."

CHAPTER SIX

The next few months were a whirl of activity. Carlos brought his wife, Carmen, and their son, Issadore, whom everyone called Issy. Issy was seven and turned out to be a great new playmate for Kurt. Juan brought his wife, Rosa, and then came ten new workmen.

Things moved quickly. It was Dan who suggested that canvas tents were hardly appropriate for Carlos's and Juan's families, or for the workmen for that matter, and suggested building wooden structures for their housing. Log cabins would go up much faster than adobe.

John and the hands cut and snaked logs from the canyon down near the stream. They built a sturdy building intended for Carlos, Juan, their wives, and Issadore.

Carlos and Juan were delighted with their new home. On Saturday night, they celebrated. They invited a band from town and many friends, along with Father Torres.

Tequila and food appeared on a long table behind the ranch house. The musicians began to play and sing, and couples danced. The workmen and their wives were dressed in their finest. The Wests and the three cowboys were amazed at the transformation.

"You see," explained Father Torres, "for six days they work very hard and then on the night of the sixth they celebrate. On Sunday, we rest and worship. Señora and Señor West, what do you think of your workmen now?"

"They measure up, they surely do,'" said John.

"I think, Father," added Priscilla, "that they have greatly enriched our lives."

"You are right; we both benefit from this friendship. Señor West, you must be very proud of your lady."

John looked thoughtfully at the priest. "Yes, I am. She's a strong woman."

"John has put up with a lot through the years," said Priscilla, "and has always kept his word to me. No woman could ask for more."

"At times, life can be sweet and a great blessing," said the priest. "I pray that these good times will continue."

John noticed Charlie, Shorty, and Dan making their way through the crowd. He nudged Priscilla and motioned for Father Torres to look up. The three cowboys had obviously dressed up. Their hair was greased back, they were smooth-shaven, and they wore their best clothes.

"Father?" asked John. "Will there be trouble?"

"Ahh, this I anticipated," answered Father Torres with a wave of his right hand. "Not long ago, I spoke with your cowboys. Shorty remained reticent, but alone with Dan and Charlie, they revealed much about their pasts. My belief is they will behave as gentlemen."

"Excuse me, Father, to make sure, I'll go and remind them."

The first Saturday fiesta at Wet Springs was a success. At the end of the party, the priest blessed them, said a short prayer, and reminded everyone that the next day was Sunday. Then the guests packed up and left for town.

The months passed quickly. Priscilla enjoyed Carmen and Rosa's company. The three women did everything together—cooked, washed dishes, and did the laundry. Punctuated with conversation and laughter, the shared work went easier. Priscilla was learning Spanish, and Carmen's and Rosa's English was improving.

Kurt and Issy became best friends. Both began to learn each other's language. Together the boys received lessons from Priscilla at the kitchen table each day.

During Father Torres's visits, John and Priscilla developed an even greater admiration. His friendship in hard times was exactly what was needed.

The building projects continued. Dan persuaded John, Shorty, and Charlie to cut and snake more logs. With the help of the other ten men, they built a long bunkhouse for the new workers to live in.

There were other benefits to the meeting of two cultures. Charlie, Shorty, and Dan each had become resigned to the fact that they would never have a wife as there were so few eligible women. The types they had known were not the ones they wanted to bring home. This changed when they met señoritas who came to the celebrations at the ranch.

Kurt, on the evening of one of the summer parties, celebrated his sixth birthday. The boy received many gifts. John bought his son a pony and a small saddle. From

Priscilla, he received several books, clothes, and leather boots. Charlie, Shorty, and Dan gave chaps, a vest, and a sombrero.

After the guests left, Kurt's father displayed a .32 pistol.

"Priscilla, this is just for the boy to learn how to shoot properly."

There was a great deal of discussion over the revolver, but what could you do with a boy who saved his father's life? Kurt was never to touch it unless an adult gave permission. It was Shorty, the best marksman among them, who volunteered to teach the boy how to shoot.

CHAPTER SEVEN

The Wests and their workers were pleased with their achievements. Priscilla did not dictate but rather shared her ideas and was open to any improvement. Carlos persuaded Priscilla to alter her plans. They dug a cellar next to the cabin and built an addition with a trap door. This room was made larger than Priscilla had originally envisioned. They now had space to store an army's worth of supplies underground. Many shelves were built, and Priscilla was satisfied.

The cabin sides were reinforced and covered with adobe. Inside, thick shutters were installed. A trap door to the roof was added, a patio with adobe walls, a front stone porch, a place to wash clothes, an outside cooking area, and the river near the house was deepened, and a dam was built.

Other improvements included a new bunkhouse for Charlie, Shorty, and Dan with separate heated rooms. A tunnel was built connecting to the house.

The last construction project was a large adobe barn where the thoroughbred mares would have a safe place to foal. It would be big enough to store hay and contain a tack room, and an outside corral.

Carlos and Juan explained they had helped build the Catholic church, and they would use the same principles to build the barn. The roof would be made of tile and be safe from fire. For such a building, it was evident they would need a massive amount of adobe bricks.

As worked progressed, it became clear that Carlos and Juan and their families were becoming a permanent part of Wet Springs. By mere accident of turning to Father Torres for help, they had gained the loyalty of new friends.

CHAPTER EIGHT

Kurt was twelve years old by the time the huge barn was finished. It was a massive structure. Carlos and Juan had completed a utilitarian building that was a work of art. The Wests felt like they were now living on a great hacienda.

Soon after the stables were completed, the thoroughbred mare was to have her fourth foal. Kurt and Shorty were in charge of the mare. So that he could watch both of them, Kurt moved his cat, Tiger, to the barn. She was going to have kittens. Shorty was disturbed—both the mare and the cat were in distress. Tiger was old, weak, and cried out. The mare must have a breech as she screamed every few minutes. Both animals were in pain.

Shorty watched Kurt as he took care of his pets. The lad went from the mare to the cat and back again. He stroked and reassured both. The boy had not eaten and had barely spoken all day. Issy came to visit but left after seeing his friend's preoccupation. Priscilla brought food and coffee to the stable. Kurt barely responded and did not eat. His mother insisted that he would either eat or return to the house—adding that he probably needed to come inside anyway. Kurt absentmindedly took a bite of a sandwich and took a few sips of the steaming black liquid.

"Ma'am," said Shorty. "If you don't mind, I sure do need Kurt's help right now. These critters seem a might more at ease with him comforting them."

Priscilla nodded and gave Kurt a tight hug. She left the barn, closing the big door quietly behind her.

Kurt continued his vigil. His heart was torn—he cared for the cat as much as he did for the mare. Past midnight the mare began to kick and scream. Kurt put both arms tightly around her lurching head and hugged her. The animal gave one long gasp, and her head dropped to the stable floor. Kurt touched her warm side—it was no longer moving. He knew she was gone. Shorty, watched in amazement as Kurt brushed the tears away with his sleeve, moved to the rear of the dead mare, and reached inside. Bracing his feet against the solid flanks, he tugged and pulled. With both hands, he slid the foal out. It was very still.

It was a filly. Kurt sat down with the wet animal over his lap. He cupped his hands around its mouth and blew air into its lungs. Nothing happened.

"Give it up, son," said Shorty. "It's too late."

There was movement, and the little filly coughed. She shook her wet head and took a deep breath.

"Where did you learn to do that?" asked the amazed Shorty.

"I don't know—guess it just came to me."

Shorty helped Kurt wipe down the fragile filly and wrap her in an old blanket. Then Tiger began to mew. The boy knelt to check on his cat. Tiger vomited. A small kitten was born. She tried to lick her kitten clean, but could not.

Tiger meowed, shuddered, and died.

Once again, Kurt swiped the back of his hand across his eyes. He picked up the wet kitten and carried it over to the foal. He sat down and gently rubbed the kitten dry with a rag. A very tiny sound escaped the kitten's mouth.

"Son," said Shorty, "they're not going to make it without their mothers."

"You're wrong!" said Kurt crossly. "They are not going to die. You go and get mother, she'll know what to do."

"Kurt, it's one o'clock in the morning. Kind of late for a man like me to be disturbing your ma."

"Alright, I'll be back."

Priscilla and John followed Kurt to the stable. John agreed with Shorty—survival did not seem possible. Priscilla, on the other hand, stated there was a slim chance if both animals were kept very warm and cared for day and night.

"I am going to take care of them, Mother. I won't let them die."

"Kurt, you would have to move to the barn and watch them twenty-four hours a day," said Priscilla. "That is a pretty big order, and most likely they still won't make it."

"If that's what it takes, I'll move out here."

"Alright. We'll need milk. Are you certain you want to do this?"

The young man nodded. Priscilla sent Shorty to find milk.

In an hour, Shorty came back. His clothes were a mess, dirty, and torn. Priscilla showed Kurt how to dip a clean rag into the liquid and let the filly suck on it. She repeated the process. She did the same with a tiny piece of cloth for the kitten. Kurt followed her example.

Shorty and John shook their heads, wished them well, and went to their beds. When Priscilla came back to the house, her husband was fast asleep. She rummaged for something to make nipples out of. Not finding anything that would work, Priscilla got dressed, strapped on a .36 cap and ball, pulled on her boots, and went to the stable. She saddled her horse and told Kurt she was going to Red Wing to get what was needed. It was a long ride. She arrived before sunup and pounded on the doctor's door. A sleepy man, wearing a nightshirt, answered her knock. Priscilla pushed herself inside and told the doctor why she was there.

"Who the blazes do you think you are coming in here like this over a couple of danged animals?" bellowed the furious man. "I am not a horse doctor."

Priscilla had not slept and was short on patience, too. "Shut up and help me or I might just feel like shooting you. I need something that will work as a bottle and nipple for a newborn filly and a tiny kitten."

The doctor calmed down when he realized just how serious this woman was."Easy, lady," he said as he cautiously backed up to a supply cupboard. He thoughtfully picked out several items, placed them in a brown paper bag, and handed it to Priscilla. "This ought to do the trick," he said as he eyed the gun at her side. "Just make certain you don't feed the critters too fast and choke them."

With what dignity she could muster, Priscilla replied.

"Doctor, I apologize for the threat. How much do I owe you?"

The physician contemplated several moments—finally, he began to laugh so hard that tears rolled down his cheeks. He wiped at his eyes. "Lady," he said, "if you don't tell anyone that you got me out of bed at the threat of gunpoint to put together a contraption to feed a kitten and filly, I won't charge you a thing. I've got a reputation to uphold—I am not a veterinarian. And, for the future, ma'am, just who are you?"

"I'm Priscilla West of Wet Springs Ranch. I am afraid I have acted in a rash and unladylike manner. Please tell me how much I owe you."

"Forget it," he smiled. "No charge for horses and cats. Now people are a different matter." The doctor laughed again.

"I am in your debt," she said as she turned to go out the door. "You are welcome to come out to our ranch and visit any time."

Priscilla rushed to her horse and rode as fast as she could towards home. She arrived on one lathered, tired-out animal. John came down to the stable and was very upset.

He began shouting, "Weren't you the one who told us never to ride alone? Weren't you the one who said never go to town without a large group for protection?"

"I apologize," said Priscilla to her angry husband. "It won't happen again."

John stood there astonished. He had never heard his wife apologize before. He watched her carry a bag into the stable. Priscilla delivered the glass dropper to Kurt. Then she took the large bottle and nipple and filled it with milk. She gave it to the filly, and it began drinking right away. She watched Kurt put milk in the dropper and place it in the kitten's tiny mouth.

"So far, so good, Kurt. You'll have to do this every two hours and remember to keep both of them warm."

"I will, Mom," said Kurt with conviction.

He cared for the orphans, day and night, for the next two weeks. The members of the ranch were fascinated. Two animals died, and their off-springs survived with the help of this young man.

CHAPTER NINE

By the fourth week, even Shorty could see the little cat and filly would live. The kitten and foal followed Kurt wherever he went. He named the kitten Little Tiger and the horse Cindy.

Kurt emerged from his isolation in the dim stable and returned to his normal routine as best he could with two animals always underfoot. They tried getting into his bedroom and sleeping there. That was fine for the cat but not for the filly. She would stomp and whinny if Kurt did not go out to her. The only solution was to put a bed in the stable and fix better-living conditions for Kurt. This was done, and one room of the stable became home to him.

Issy and Kurt continued with their studies. Shorty not only still gave shooting lessons to Kurt, but also to Issy.

Juan and Carlos were asked if they would like to learn to shoot—Juan declined. However, Carlos had always wanted to be a cowboy.

It was at this time that things began to disintegrate. John, Shorty, and Charlie rode into Red Wing to pay the taxes on the ranch. They were turned back from the courthouse by Poindexter's men. Rather than face overwhelming odds, the Wests departed, as was Poindexter's intent.

Not long after that, several snipers fired down on the ranch from high ground. These attacks made daily routines difficult and dangerous. Five of the ten workers who helped construct the buildings quit. The other five agreed to remain, and Carlos taught them how to ride and shoot.

The following Saturday, several Mexicans and their families coming to the ranch for the fiesta were attacked. They were roped and dragged by cowboys. Two of the workers and one of their wives were injured. This ended the Saturday night festivities.

The terror escalated, even more, when Poindexter's men shot, dragged and murdered two of the Mexican hands. The last three workers quit. Everyone else on the ranch took up pistol and rifle practice.

Then began a time of siege. The residents of the ranch performed their chores while armed. Kurt wore a .38 caliber pistol on his right side and a matched pistol on his left hip for a cross draw. No one except Shorty really knew that the best shot and the quickest draw was Kurt. He had been practicing almost every day for six years.

Very early one morning, Dan and Charlie got up and saddled their horses. They rode back into the fenced canyon to check on the herd. A cattle drive would have to be made in the fall. The Wests had recently sold a few steers cheaply and secretly to the Mexican community. Priscilla had given two more to Father Torres to feed the poor in town. Poindexter was making it very hard on the Spanish speaking people.

That day, when Charlie and Dan went back into the

canyon to check on the cattle, they were alarmed to discover some of the fence posts had been pulled sideways; it looked as if someone had tried to let the herd out. That was the last thing Charlie or Dan ever saw. A fusillade of shots echoed through the canyon and up to the ranch house. Charlie was shot in the head, and bullets riddled his body. Dan tried to pull his pistol, and he was shot in his chest. They were both dead before they hit the ground.

John, watering horses, heard the shooting, and yelled, "Shorty, get the Sharps."

John, Shorty, Carlos, Issy, and Kurt ran to the stable, saddled their horses, and rode straight for the canyon. A hundred yards from the fence, they stopped. Shorty looked through the Sharps' scope.

"Boss, it looks like a bunch of men are pulling down the fence posts. Guess we built em good, cause they're not having much success."

"What do you suggest, Shorty?"

"I don't see Dan and Charlie, but I do see two men on the ground. Let's leave the horses and move closer. When you hear me fire this Sharps, empty those rifles."

They ran using the existing ground cover as best they could. At times Shorty stopped and waited. They came within fifty feet without being seen. It was a very effective range for rifles. They lay flat and waited. Kurt was carrying two rifles. Shorty aimed, and the Sharps went off, and the leader of the group went down.

Kurt, John, and Carlos fired at their targets and emptied their rifles. There was some sporadic return fire, but it soon ended. The bullets were going in one direction, and that was from the Wet Springs rifles.

"Come on," shouted Shorty. "Let's go."

The tough, little, bowlegged man ran as fast as he could, leading the charge, both of his pistols out. When he got close enough, he started blazing away. Kurt followed his example and downed two escaping riders.

"Careful!" yelled John.

They eased up to the fence and looked at the bodies sprawled across the ground. Some were dead, others dying. One rider wearing a checked shirt raised a pistol.

"Look out, Dad!" yelled Kurt, he jumped in front of his father and fired.

"Boss," exclaimed Shorty. "Those varmints shot Charlie and Dan. My pards!"

His stomach lurched as he stared down at Charlie. Several wounded rustlers were on the ground moaning.

"Moan, you vermin!" shouted Shorty. "Moan and go to the devil!"

Shorty ran to a man holding his shoulder and pointed his pistol.

"Reach, coward, or so help me I'll shoot you now."

John gripped his ranch hand's arm. "Shorty, you can't do it, no matter how much you want to."

Shorty went limp, holstered his pistols, and stood motionless.

Carlos, Kurt, and John began gathering weapons and frisking bodies.

One man groaned and whispered, "Shorty, don't you know me? Bill Carpenter—your old saddle-mate."

"Yeah?"

"Poindexter thought he had you beat and that you were easy pickins. He got that wrong. I'm..." Carpenter choked and fell back.

"Dead and none too soon," said Shorty.

John went up to a man holding his shoulder, "You want to live or not?" he demanded.

"Water! Can I have some water?" the man whispered."

"Not until you tell us who you work for?"

"Poindexter."

"Who ordered this raid on my ranch?"

"He did," the wounded man pointed to Bill Carpenter.

"What was the plan?"

"To rustle your cattle and mix them in with Poindexter's herd."

"Why did you shoot my men?"

"Our orders were to kill anybody on sight."

"Will you tell the judge that?"

"If I do, I won't live long."

"And if you don't," replied John, "I promise you'll bleed to death."

"Help me, and I'll talk."

"Kurt, go to the ranch and send back your mother. Make sure she has bandages for four.

"Alright, Dad."

"Wait, Kurt, there's more. You and Issy harness up two wagons and bring them out here. Hurry!"

Issy and Kurt caught two of the outlaw's horses.

Reaching the ranch, Kurt ran to the house and found his mother. Priscilla was already preparing bandages. She took one of the saddled horses and rode to the canyon. Issy and Kurt went to the barn. They each harnessed horses to two separate wagons and started back.

When they reached the fence, they saw Priscilla taking care of the wounded.

"Boys," said John, "Put the weapons in one of the wagons. Then chase down the rustler's horses. We'll take the ones with Poindexter's brand to town. Let the sheriff and judge try to deny this."

Priscilla finished bandaging the four men.

"One will die for certain," she told her husband, "two should recover, and one—I don't know."

She went over to where Charlie and Dan lay. Kneeling down, she gently touched each man. Tears rolled down her cheeks. *Such kind and wonderful men so senselessly killed.*

Carlos and John struggled with the grisly business of loading the dead bodies onto one of the wagons. Shorty was sitting on the ground, too broken up to help. Priscilla went to one of the wagons, took two blankets that were used for seat cushions, and brought them back and covered the bodies of Charlie and Dan. Then Carlos and John carried them to the empty wagon.

"I'll be darned if I'll let Charlie and Dan ride with those dead devils," exclaimed John.

Priscilla took Shorty's arm, urged him up.

"The three of us been pards as long as I remember," said Shorty. "What am I going to do now?"

"Take care of us," said Priscilla.

Shorty got up on the wagon seat. Carlos and John

hoisted the four wounded prisoners up beside Charlie and Dan. Priscilla drove the first wagon to the ranch. Carlos took the other wagon with the dead outlaws.

John went to help Issy and Kurt gather the rustlers' horses. They captured eleven.

John stood near the fence to the canyon. The large wooden posts were tilted sideways and would have to be fixed. It was clear the only thing that had prevented the Poindexter gang from stealing the cattle was Charlie's insistence that a blacksmith forge a heavy gate. This was attached to metal posts stuck deep in the ground. Two enormous chains and locks held the gate in place. The outlaws were simply unable to budge the solid fence.

At the ranch, Priscilla fought tears as she tried not to think about Charlie and Dan. They had been family, not just hands. She knew for the sake of the rest of them, she had to focus on what needed to be done now. She started making plans, and she was anxious to discuss them with her husband and Carlos. She hoped Shorty would be recovered enough to listen. By the time John got back, he had already come up with a plan of his own. He knew what needed to be done.

John, Kurt, and Issy rode up behind the cabin and got down. The two wagons and horses were with Carlos, who was guarding the prisoners.

"Kurt, Issy," said John. "Check the brands. The ones with Poindexter's I want tied to the back of the wagon behind the dead men. Put the remainder in the corral. I want the saddles and saddlebags stripped off and placed in the tack room. Bring the rifles and pistols to the house.

Hurry, no time to waste!"

With a determined step, John went into the ranch house. Priscilla opened her mouth to speak.

"Priscilla, I've taken a back seat for a lot of years, now it's my turn."

"John," she responded, "I get my say, remember?"

"Priscilla, will you let me talk, just this once?"

She glared at him. "All right, John."

He nodded and continued, "We have the evidence we need. The horses with Poindexter's brand we can show the sheriff and the judge. We've got dead outlaws people can identify as Poindexter's men. And, we've got the man with the wounded arm, willing to testify that Poindexter's foreman, Carpenter, told them to raid the ranch, steal the cattle, and shoot anyone on site. Any problems so far, Priscilla?"

"No, John."

"Are you with us, Shorty?" John asked his old friend. "They shot Charlie and Dan, and that's murder. We'll go to town and help the Sheriff arrest Poindexter and put him in jail for trial."

"It'll never work," growled Shorty. "A few years ago maybe, but now Poindexter owns the town. What he says goes. He's the law now."

"I hope you're wrong, Shorty," replied John. "We'll go in armed and ready. Will you try anyway?

Shorty sat at the kitchen table in a wicked mood. He was in a state of shock about his friends, and his anger burned for revenge. "Yeah, I'm with you. What about Charlie and Dan? What are you going to do for them?"

John looked at his wife.

"Shorty," said Priscilla, "we'll take them into town on the wagon, and Father Torres will give them a good funeral."

Shorty was so upset he was shaking. "Yes ma'am, that would be about as good as old Charlie and Dan can expect. It'll be fine to see two good caskets, candles, and holy water and such. Only, I want to be there and see them put my pards in the ground."

"It'll be dangerous," said John.

"No never mind; they're not going into the ground unless I'm there to see them off."

"Alright, Shorty," replied John. "Let's pack up whatever provisions we might need. I think Carlos, Kurt, Priscilla, you, and I should go. Juan, Issy, and the women need to stay and guard the ranch. Priscilla?"

"Alright, John," replied the wife.

"I have a strange feeling they're not expecting us," said John. "They think they beat us."

Issy and Kurt brought in the side-arms and long guns. "They may have been low on brainpower, but they sure bought the best," said Kurt."

"Issy, will you go out and relieve your father and ask him to come in here?" asked John.

In a moment, Carlos came through the door. John explained what they had decided and asked if he would go. Carlos looked at his wife.

"Yes, Señor, I will go with you."

"It's now or never," said John. "Alright, everyone grab whatever you need."

The members of the ranch rifled through the large array of weapons. Shorty had no interest in the armory on the floor; his pistols were a matched set that he had carried for years.

Now fully armed, the Wet Springs crew walked out the door. The group placed filled canteens and food on the front seat. Boxes of ammunition went on the floor of the wagon. Juan and Carlos had already loaded the bandaged prisoners onto the lumpy tarp of the second wagon. The live prisoners complained about having to ride the 20 miles sitting on their dead comrades.

Carlos and Juan carried the wrapped bodies of Charlie and Dan and put them on the tarp right next to the prisoners. When the wounded squawked, Shorty, pulled a pistol. They shut up.

Issy and Kurt had five saddled Wet Spring's horses waiting, each one bearing rifles and scabbards on the sides of their saddles. Carlos tied his horse to the back of the wagon next to a line of eight Poindexter mounts. He got up on the seat and followed the first wagon towards the town of Red Wing.

Slowed by the heavily loaded wagon, it took six hours to travel the twenty miles. About halfway, they stopped; the living took on food and water. In a grim mood, they continued on. They arrived at eight o'clock that Sunday evening. Turning off the main road, the wagons and horses headed for the Mexican section of town. There was some kind of activity at the Episcopalian Church, and as they passed, singing and the throaty sound of an organ filtered out into the evening air.

They pulled up to the Catholic Church, and Carlos talked to someone in Spanish. He asked him to get the priest. Father Torres came out short of breath.

"What is it I can do for Señor and Señora West?" the priest asked.

Priscilla gave him a brief version of the story. Embellishments came from Carlos, John, and Kurt. Shorty just sat on his horse looking like a stunned rattler.

"So, under this tarp are the dead men? Who will bury them?" asked the priest.

"Poindexter will, or the town, whether they like it or not," said John.

"You plan to take these men and this wagon to the sheriff and ask him to arrest Señor Poindexter?"

"That's the plan."

"I am afraid, John West, that you will find that the sheriff, the judge, and most of the town is on Poindexter's side. What you propose involves danger."

"We know, Father."

"The answer I want from you, priest," growled Shorty coming out of a dazed stupor. "Are you going to bury my pards or not?"

"Señor Shorty?"

"No Señor, just plain Shorty."

"Yes Shorty, we will take your friends..."

"The snakes killed my pards, Charlie and Dan. They just plain out murdered them; they never had a chance."

"It is a terrible thing," said the priest. "Lo siento muchisimo! Señores Charlie and Dan were very good men".

"Yes, the best!" said Shorty, "That skunk Poindexter is going to pay. We want to see them buried right—with the holy fixins."

"Of course," said Father Torres. "We will do our best to honor them. They will have a church service and flowers at the grave. For the headstones, you can instruct what to inscribe. They will be buried in our cemetery where you can visit. Is that what you wish, Shorty?"

The cowboy blinked and shook his head as if having trouble seeing. He got down from his horse and approached Father Torres. Shorty put rough hands to the priest's shoulders and squeezed hard.

"I never talked to no priest before. I steered clear of you at the ranch. You make me ashamed."

Father Torres raised a hand to the cowhand's chest.

"Is there anything more I can do?" asked the priest.

"Yes, I want to be there."

"Of course, tomorrow at ten o'clock we will have the service. You will remain here as one of us."

Father Torres said something in Spanish to a man standing near the church. The fellow hurried away. Within a few minutes, he returned with sandals, a straw sombrero, pants, shirt, and serape. They were tied in a bundle and set on the wagon seat. Father Torres spoke to four other men. One at a time, Charlie and Dan were taken off the wagon, and four Mexicans carried them down an alley.

"Caskets will be made," explained Father Torres.

Shorty went to the church steps and sat down. Priscilla and John came forward to speak with the priest.

"I suggest that you approach the sheriff cautiously," said

the Father. "I am afraid he will not help you. His loyalty is to Poindexter. I am certain you will find him very hostile. It is good that today is Sunday, not many of Poindexter's gunmen will be in town."

"Thank you for the advice, Father," said John

"Via con Dios."

At a signal from John, Carlos drove the wagon towards the sheriff's office, and the Wet Springs crew followed. Before the office, Shorty stopped John.

"I guess this is the time to tell you," grumbled Shorty. "In the old days, I was a gun-hand. When I met up with old Dan and Charlie, I changed my name. What I'm getting at is that I taught your boy to shoot. Youngster or not, he's the best I've ever seen. I reckon you ought to know since we may be getting into somethin we might not be able to get out of."

There was a moment of awkward silence.

"Thanks, Shorty," said John. "We've known for a long time that Kurt can do things beyond his age."

"Saying that," said Shorty, "I think Kurt and I should go into the sheriff's office with you."

Priscilla started to object, and John gave her a look that stopped her.

Sheriff Engler, a short round fellow with a puffy face, was seated at his desk as Kurt stepped inside the office. The sheriff had yellow skin and looked sickly. His close-set eyes and stern features made him look all the more intimidating.

"No one else here, Dad," called Kurt as he stood just inside the open door of the office.

"What's this about?" growled the sheriff looking beyond Kurt and out the window. "Say, what are those men doing on that wagon? What's under the tarp? And what are all those horses doing tied up like that?"

"If you'll stop, I'll tell you, Engler," replied John West stepping into the office.

John explained in crisp short sentences the attack on Wet Springs Ranch. He led the Sheriff outside and showed him Bill Carpenter, the other dead men, and the horses with Poindexter's brand. He directed Engler to the wounded prisoner who confessed that Poindexter was behind the raid.

"That's it," said John. "We'll help you arrest Poindexter and go get the judge."

"How do I know you didn't cook this here deal up? Looks like to me I could get you for murder and horse stealing."

The sheriff went for his gun, and Shorty was there to tonk him on the head. Down he went.

"So much for that," said John.

"Told you so," said Shorty.

"Now what will we do?" asked Priscilla.

"Go find the judge and try this again."

They grabbed the unconscious sheriff and tied his hands behind his back with leather thongs. Kurt and Shorty threw him in back of the wagon with the wounded.

"Hey," said the one with the wounded arm, "a fellow back here just died."

"Good," said Shorty. "One less to worry about."

Shorty led them back past the Catholic Church and

stopped. "I know where the judge's house is," he said. "Kurt, you go to the door. We'll see what goes from there."

Kurt and Shorty rode their horses down the street and turned the corner. Shorty led him past the house and stopped. Kurt took off his guns and hung them on the saddle horn. Shorty waited around the side of the house while Kurt knocked.

A servant came to the door. Kurt, looking every bit of his twelve years, asked for the judge. The female servant informed the innocent-looking boy that the judge and his wife were at the church for a special service honoring Mr. Poindexter.

Kurt came back to the horses, took his guns down from the saddle horn, and put them on.

"Did you hear that? Honoring that murderer?" said Kurt.

"Yeah."

"Now what do we do?"

"I don't know. Let's go tell the others."

Standing near the loaded wagon, they discussed their options. They knew the inside of the church well and the locations of the exits and entrances. There were three: double doors up front, a side exit, and a back door. They decided John and Priscilla would enter with the sheriff through the front. Shorty and Carlos would take the side exit, and Kurt would come in through the back.

Shorty pointed out, "This won't be no picnic." Poindexter is sure to have armed men with him. We have to be ready. Tricky thing to shoot in a crowded church."

"Maybe we should wait," said Priscilla.

"We're taking a risk," said Shorty. "but if we leave now we're going to be labeled as crooks. Best we air this in public and tell our side of the story. Who knows what they'll think up against us after we leave."

"What choice do we have?" asked John. "We need to convince the townspeople. Seeing the evidence, a few might change their minds. They already branded us as outlaws. If we show them proof, at least they will see what Poindexter's doing with their own eyes."

"Alright, John," said Shorty. "You take the bull by the horns and run the show. Kurt, I figure if it comes to shooting, I can get one or two, but not all of Poindexter's guards. Your mother and father aren't too handy, but you are."

Kurt looked at his mother and then met his father's eyes. How young the boy gunfighter looked.

"Yes," Kurt said. "I'll cover you."

Kurt and Shorty tied the man with the wounded arm to the seat of the wagon. The other two wounded men weren't going anywhere. John and Priscilla threw water in the face of the unconscious sheriff. He awoke, and John began to push him toward the church. The plan was simple. Go near the entrance, wait two minutes until everyone was in position and then go in.

Kurt, Carlos, and Shorty ran to the back and side entrances of the church and carefully made their way inside without being observed. They waited until John and Priscilla, with the sheriff in tow, came through the double doors. When they did, the three men entered the sanctuary. Kurt came down through the vestry and stopped just below the altar in the center aisle. Carlos ran across in front of Kurt and went to the right aisle; Shorty stayed on the far left side.

The preacher, Reverend Pellett, was standing in the pulpit. He stopped as John and Priscilla dragged Sheriff Engler down the middle aisle. They halted next to Poindexter. The land-grabber arose from his seat. He was tall and slim, his pale skin dry as parchment. His face looked cadaverous, and it was impossible to tell how old he was. He wore a suit and tie that obviously had not come from the local mercantile. His expressionless, beady eyes, stared at the Wests. The church was deadly quiet when he finally began speaking in a low menacing voice.

"So, the rustlers and the Mexican lovers have abducted our sheriff and come to intrude on my tribute. Or, perhaps, you have finally seen the light and have come to offer terms."

Shorty with slight hand signals pointed out which of the persons in the room were Poindexter's guards. It wasn't difficult, as each armed man had stood up when the Wests burst in. There were two guards on Shorty's side—two in front of Kurt and one near Carlos and the side door. Five gunmen altogether.

"A lying speech from a rustler and a low-down land-grabber," replied John West. "As for your slur about Mexicans, the lowliest worker has more integrity in his little finger than you do in your entire body. This time we have undeniable proof."

"Judge, Judge Baxter, are you here?" John called, looking out over the open-mouthed congregation.

A very fat, well-dressed man with snow white hair stood up. "I'm here."

"Judge, we're going to have a trial. We've got dead rustlers, Poindexter's branded horses, and a live witness."

"Guards!" yelled Poindexter. "Shoot them!"

The crooked rancher's men began to draw their weapons. Shorty, Kurt, and Carlos drew theirs. Members of the crowd screamed and ducked. With one hand John jerked the stumbling sheriff in front of Priscilla and drew one of his pistols with the other.

Kurt, without hesitation, identified his two targets. He shot the first guard in his gunhand, and the man's pistol dropped. Explosions of simultaneous gunfire echoed deafeningly off the walls of the church. Women screamed. A gunman at the back of the room leveled two pistols at Kurt. Kurt shot both of the man's shoulders before the other guard could fire. Two revolvers fell to the floor.

A third guard shot at John West standing behind the sheriff and the bullet nicked the rancher's shirt. Shorty shot the man in the hand, and the pistol flew against a pew and dropped. A fourth Poindexter man took aim and fired. Shorty winced from a bullet-graze in his side. Kurt fired twice hitting the gunman's hand and leg. The gunfighter fell.

Carlos, with knees and hand shaking, aimed his pistol towards the last guard standing on his side of the aisle. Saying a "Hail Mary," he blasted away. The guard shot Carlos in the left leg, and he went down. From a sitting position, steadying the pistol with both hands, Carlos fired, wounding, but not killing the guard.

The deafening noise ended but still echoed in the ears of the congregation. People were screaming and fighting to flatten themselves onto the floor. Others in the pews were pushing, trying to escape. It was chaos. When the gunfire ended, there was a brief moment of complete silence.

Calmly, Kurt moved around picking up weapons from Poindexter's wounded crew. Remarkably, no one from Wet Springs was killed.

After Kurt stacked the weapons near Shorty, he gave his friend a kerchief to help stop the bleeding. Kurt went to Carlos, took the ranch hands colorful bandanna, and wrapped it around the hole in Carlos's leg. Kurt saw Dr. Bennett, who was just starting toward one of the wounded gunmen.

In tardy indignation, Reverend Pellett yelled out, "No shooting in the church, please!"

"Little late for that, Pellett," mocked John.

"This is a house of God," protested the preacher.

"You mean it was," replied Priscilla. "It's questionable how Godly it is when you let the devil in. Of course, you know that you're sitting and consorting with him." She motioned toward Poindexter, "He's not even man enough to do his own dirty work. He hires others to do it for him. Then he comes to church and acts as if he has nothing to do with his dirty schemes."

Priscilla nodded to her husband for him to continue.

"Okay, Judge Baxter," said John, "let's talk about this trial."

"There will be none here," said Judge Baxter rising from a pew. "You are the ones who will be on trial for attacking, without cause, Mr. Poindexter and his hands."

"That does it," said John. "Has everyone in this town sold out? Let's try this another way. Poindexter, you're a coward and a murderer; you hired gunslingers to harass and kill innocent ranch owners and to rustle their cattle. You intimidate honest citizens, and you steal land. You hide behind gunmen and shoot anyone who does not cooperate with you. You're so crooked you can't think or walk straight—so rotten you stink from the inside out. You're a filthy liar and a cheat. Now pick up a gun and let's go outside and settle it, man to man."

Poindexter glared but didn't answer. He just looked at Judge Baxter for a sign of his allegiance.

"Alright," said John. "Since you are too afraid to face me, let's try something else."

John went over and slapped Poindexter hard across the face. Poindexter's eyes narrowed like that of a rattlesnake. John hit him harder. Blood trickled out of Poindexter's nose and mouth. Still, the man did not speak or move.

"You don't have any guts at all." John threw Poindexter a pistol. "Pick it up."

Poindexter remained still.

"I can't hear you, Poindexter. Pick it up, or I…I'll beat you to a pulp!"

"Now, is not the time," mumbled Poindexter through swollen lips.

"What does that mean?"

"What he means, dear husband," said Priscilla, "is that he's going to wait until we leave and then he's going to send an army of men to get us. Isn't that right, Poindexter?"

"I'd like to see you prove that accusation," he sneered as he daintily wiped his nose and lips.

Priscilla, angered beyond endurance, picked up her husband's pistol that was lying on the floor, drew back the hammer, and aimed at Poindexter's head.

"Listen to me!" said Priscilla. "This coward has committed so many acts of murder and theft. Here is our opportunity to get rid of this abomination. We have the evidence. How many will stand up and support us?"

No one rose from the pews. For the first time, Priscilla noticed that sitting next to Poindexter was his wife and his daughter Penelope.

"I'm sorry, Mrs. Poindexter," said Priscilla. "We don't hold you responsible for things your husband does. It must be a real hardship."

"It sure is," said Penelope cutting her mother short.

"Shut up, you hussy," snarled Poindexter.

"You're not my father," said Penelope. "Everything these people say about you is true."

Despite the pistol to his head, the crooked rancher managed to backhand his stepdaughter.

"Why you," said Priscilla angrily.

She took the pistol and struck Poindexter across the face. He reeled against the church pew.

"Who will stand up and join us?" asked Priscilla. "You heard the girl; even a member of his own family hates him. Who will make a jury of twelve so we can have a trial and hang him? If you don't, soon none of you will be safe."

"I'll stand behind you," echoed a voice from across the room. "Lord knows, I don't have anything to be scared of.

If someone gives me a long gun, I'll back you. The name's Jedidiah Taylor."

"Oldtimer, you won't regret this," said John West.

"Real Christian of you. You folks got sand. Reminds me of the old days."

"Who else?" John's eyes scanned the room.

"I'll stand behind you," said Dr. Bennett. "I know this lady, and so do you. I heard how she nursed many of you during the epidemic. Shame on you folks. We know who the scoundrel is."

"Better sit down, Bennett, before you get yourself killed," said Judge Baxter. "Don't go judging us until you know the facts."

"What facts?" asked the doctor. "That you would rather go on living as cowards? Better have a trial now and get rid of this man."

"Thank you, doctor," said Priscilla. "By the way, the mare and kitten lived."

"I was mighty pleased to be of service."

The doctor went back to caring for some of the wounded gunmen.

"Surely there are others who will stand with us," said Priscilla.

Mrs. Schmidt started to rise, but her husband pushed her down. Priscilla nodded and smiled at her friend.

Silence came to the room, and no one moved.

"That's it," said Shorty. "Boss, let's just shoot the polecat."

"Can't do it, Shorty. Much as we would like to. We're not like him."

"Then let me tell you, good folks, what this son-of-the-devil did," exclaimed Shorty. "He sent his foreman Bill Carpenter over to our ranch with twelve gunmen to rustle our cattle. Charlie and Dan never had a chance. Killed in cold blood. I'll prove it. Kurt, go get that Poindexter man."

After a few minutes, Kurt brought in the wounded rustler. All eyes turned to Poindexter's gunman.

"Now talk!" said Shorty.

Hesitantly the rustler, hands tied behind his back, told the congregation what he and the others did at Wet Springs Ranch.

"Now," said Shorty, "the rest of you are going outside and see those dead outlaws and the string of Poindexter horses. For twelve years Poindexter has been harassing the Wests. You folks are fools if you don't put Poindexter under. Cause if the law don't work for us, then it won't work for you."

Shorty began lifting church members from a pew and pushing them towards the double doors. The rest of the congregation rose and filed out. Mrs. West had a gun in Poindexter's back and was pushing him along. Kurt had cut back the tarp, and the onlookers could easily see the grisly figures. They also witnessed Poindexter's brand on the eight horses.

"What now, Boss?" asked Shorty.

"I don't know," said John. "Judge Baxter, do we have enough evidence to hang Poindexter?"

"I can't say."

"Then what can you say?" demanded John. "What hold does that man have over you?"

"Such impertinence!" sputtered the angry judge.

"Can't handle the truth?" retorted John. "If you represent the law, why don't you act?"

"If there is a trial, John West," said the judge, "it is you who will be tried. Those bodies are in your possession. You are the one who looks guilty."

"Go to Hades, Judge," returned John. "You're just as crooked as Poindexter."

"Folks," shouted Shorty. "You can have the dead ones and the live ones, and the blood-soaked wagon, cause we sure in the heck don't want 'em."

Priscilla took her pistol and struck the back of Poindexter's head, and the man fell.

"You can have this crook!" she yelled to the bystanders.

Kurt helped Carlos get on his horse, and the five members of Wet Springs started out of town.

A voice could be heard yelling behind them, "Hey, thar! Hold up!" Old man Jedidiah came loping forward with an old Spencer rifle and a strapped-on cap and ball pistol. He untied one of Poindexter's horses and climbed up on the wagon, pulling the horse beside it. He stood on a dead man, swung his leg over the side of the wagon, and mounted the horse bareback. He kicked his heels, and the old man rode the horse out of town toward the Wests.

He caught up with the five from Wet Springs and pulled up.

"Went powerful well, considering."

"Considering what, old-timer?" asked John.

"Considering you didn't kill nobody. Why in my day..."

The old man started talking about his past exploits and

didn't stop.

"Old man," said Shorty, "hold that mouth of yours and give us some air."

"All you had to do was ask," replied Jedidiah.

Coming to a pile of rocks, Shorty and Kurt dismounted. This was where they would camp the night. It was a hidden place to sleep and picket horses until the funeral in the morning.

"I'm going to stay with Shorty," said Kurt. "I want to be there to say good-bye to Charlie and Dan."

"We don't want you to take the risk, Son," said Priscilla.

"We've been taking risks for a long time now, Mom. Can't talk me out of it. I'll get up early and ride in with Shorty and get some proper clothes from Father Torres. You forget that I can speak Spanish."

"And you forget, Son, that you have blue eyes and blond hair. But, if you insist, you keep covered, and you stay with Shorty."

They left the two behind. John, Priscilla, and the wounded Carlos, who was in great pain, along with the old man, headed for the ranch.

CHAPTER TEN

In the morning before sunup, Shorty woke Kurt and they drank water and ate jerky. Shorty was wearing sandals, loose cotton pants, shirt, and a serape. When he put on the floppy brimmed sombrero, the costume was complete. They rode to a secluded area near the church and stopped. Mexican villagers came forward. Leaving their horses, they entered the back of the church. Kurt was given an outfit, and he quickly changed clothes. Father Torres smiled at their costumes.

"Señor Kurt, Shorty, you are now one of us. Please come to my humble chambers, and we will eat and talk."

They followed the priest to a room with a large table. They were given frijoles and coffee.

"The town is talking of your exploits from yesterday. This Poindexter—shall we say—woke up from your mother's 'persuasiveness' and he was like a hornet, no, a great mad bull. Right now there is much activity in the town. Many gunmen are acquiring supplies and ammunition. I am afraid they intend to make a raid on your ranch. It will be dangerous returning to Wet Springs. I would suggest keeping the clothes. Perhaps they will help disguise both of you when you leave."

"Thank you for your help and kindness, Father," said Kurt.

"My pleasure, my son. My people are honored. Is it true you used your pistols last night?"

"Yes, Father."

"You are a brave boy, no, a remarkable young man. Shorty, the funeral will start at ten o'clock. I hope you will be pleased."

"Charlie and Dan deserve a good send-off. They were good men."

"I am sure they were, and I will say so in the service."

"Father Torres, there is something more that I need to ask you," said Kurt.

"Yes, go ahead."

"In the past you have helped my parents to sell cattle. We have several hundred head that have to be moved out of the canyon before they are rustled or overgraze the grass. Is there a way that you can help us to find a buyer? We would sell them at a fair price. The thing is, the buyer would have to come and get the cattle and be willing to fight Poindexter's men for them. I've been thinking that the vaqueros in Mexico could handle such a situation. Or, maybe some of the Spanish ranchos would be willing to come and take our cattle."

"Yes, it would take men who are willing to fight Poindexter. Vaqueros are good with cattle and are much capable of handling rustlers. I think we will find some of our people to do this. The price must be cheap enough. Are you authorized to make a quote, Señor Kurt?"

Kurt looked at Shorty. He had not thought quite this far.

"Don't look at me, you started this," said Shorty. "Now finish it."

"I would ask you, Father, to help us get the best price. Cattle are going for thirty-three dollars at the railhead. I was thinking, we would not go lower than fifteen dollars. That should be incentive enough for the vaqueros to come north."

"Yes, I will try for more than fifteen dollars a head, but no less than that amount. I will tell them to come at night and be prepared for danger. The number again—two hundred steers?"

"Yes, about that, Father."

"Then, after the funeral I shall send a messenger. As soon as I hear, you will be notified. The men who come shall hoot like an owl, and you will know they are friendly."

"Father," said Shorty. "It sounds as if you have done this before."

"Shorty, a priest takes on many duties in this land where we are ruled by others. Anything to help my people and our friends."

Father Torres got up and led Shorty and Kurt to the sanctuary where the bodies of their friends lay. The priest left the two of them alone until ten o'clock. Charlie and Dan were lying in rest near the altar. The wooden caskets were open. The reposed had their hair neatly combed, their faces rouged and powdered. By some magic, the bullet holes were filled, and Charlie and Dan looked almost as if they were sleeping.

Incense wafted through the air. The sweet aroma of

flowers came from large clusters arranged and placed on the ends of the caskets.

The Father came in wearing priestly robes. With two altar boys beside him, he began the service. Shorty looked behind him, and half the pews were filled with neatly dressed people attending the service. All this for his Charlie and Dan. The priest was more than keeping his word. Never had Shorty been filled with such gratitude toward his fellow man.

The priest came and stood before Shorty and told the congregation that he would give the final epitaph in English. And, to the surprise of Shorty and Kurt, the priest revealed that both Dan and Charlie were both raised in the Catholic Church as children, a confidence not even their best friend Shorty had known.

Father Torres gave a sermon about good and evil, about struggle and conflict. "In this world," said Father Torres, "there are some who live with evil in their hearts. No matter what they have, whatever the day brings, it is never enough; they are never satisfied, and certainly never grateful. But thankfully, there are also those who live with love. Good people who understand that every minute, every hour of every day is singular. They see with open eyes God's gifts, birds of the air, the grass and flowers of the fields, the sunrise and sunset. These believers recognize it is all special. They realize every moment of life on earth is a gift to be cherished.

"I had the privilege of meeting and knowing Charlie and Dan. I know these were two men who recognized that life is unique. In this realization, Charlie and Dan gave of themselves to those around them. To their pal, Shorty, to their bosses Señor and Señora West, to Kurt and everyone else they met and liked. They were full of the love of life, not of hate and death. They were not takers; they were givers. They were not evil but good.

"So, in remembering Charlie and Dan, we regret their passing even as we celebrate their earthly lives. We mourn and weep over their loss on this earth and pray for their passing souls into a better life. In the Name of the Father, the Son, and the Holy Ghost, Amen."

Both Shorty and Kurt were deeply moved and wished that the rest of the Wet Springs crew could have been there. What pain Poindexter and his men had caused.

A beautiful alto voice accompanied by one guitar began to sing. It was a lovely and mournful Spanish tune. When the song finished, the congregation came, bowed in respect, and filed away.

After the service, Father Torres motioned for Shorty and Kurt to follow him. They went out through the side of the church into a fenced graveyard; the place was like a garden with flowers and statues. The congregation walked in a long procession to two newly dug graves. They stood, with Shorty and Kurt in front, and waited for the caskets that were carried by six men each. The rest of the ceremony went quickly, and Shorty watched as the men lowered the caskets into the graves. Soon it was time to file past and say a final goodbye. Shorty picked up a handful of dirt and sifted it through his fingers onto each coffin. He stopped and picked up two flowers and dropped one onto each casket.

Shorty hadn't had a dry eye the entire time. He went back to the priest and told the father he was a man of his word and whatever the ranch hand could ever do for him, he would do it. The priest said he understood and shook hands. Then Kurt and Shorty turned and followed a boy to their horses.

The older gunfighter led his young friend around the back of town, through thick brush, and then due west. He figured that they might escape Poindexter's men if they took a roundabout way by riding past the ranch and then approaching it from the east. This was a direction few ever traveled. It would involve riding through brush, gullies, and rocks. Shorty couldn't ever recall traveling this way himself.

A few miles away from the ranch, at exactly three o'clock in the afternoon, Shorty and Kurt rode up on seventeen of Poindexter's men. They were sitting on horses getting ready to ride for a four o'clock raid on Wet Springs. Seeing two Mexicans ride towards them did not unduly startle the gunmen. The leader approached.

"What are you Mex doing out here? Say, that's the Wet Springs brand!"

The Poindexter man's horse turned nervously while the leader drew his revolver. Kurt jumped down, threw back his serape, drew his six-gun and shot the raider. The other gunmen reacting, pulled their revolvers, and in the noise and excitement, horses pranced and turned recklessly making shots go wild. With the reins in one hand and six-gun in the other, young Kurt stood sideways as Shorty had taught him and calmly aimed, shot, and emptied saddles.

Shorty stared in wonder at Kurt's calm demeanor during the deadly gunfight. The older Wet Springs hand struggled to control his mount. Dust rose from prancing hooves and visibility lessoned. Catching on, Shorty jumped down, held the bridle in his left hand and fired. Both of the Wet Springs hands were now accurately shooting raiders down from their frantic mounts. In fear, some of the other riders, still seated on excited horses, rode away. Others returned inaccurate fire. One rider shot and hit Kurt's range horse in the head. The mustang fell.

Kurt holstered his empty pistol, made a right-hand cross draw and continued firing. With each shot, a saddle was emptied. Some of the outlaws were now steadying their horses. Kurt dove to cover behind his dead horse. The outlaws' shooting intensified.

"Shorty! Get down behind my horse before you get shot!"

The little man let go of his reins, came running and slid behind the dead animal. Bullets made whumping sounds as they hit horseflesh. Kurt and Shorty snapped accurate shots at the circling outlaws. If any of them had been smart enough to get on the ground, they might have hit something. As it was, Kurt and Shorty were still alive only because they had made a stand.

There were now more bodies on the ground than in the saddle. The remainder of the outlaws rode away. Kurt jerked a .44 Winchester from the saddle-sheath of the dead horse and gave it to Shorty. With a rifle, the older cowboy was a deadly marksman. Bullets burned the backs of several escaping riders.

Shorty stood up and so did the boy gunfighter. Kurt began reloading his other pistol. Shorty walked around and counted bodies. Many outlaws were dead, those still breathing were gasping their last breaths—one was crying in pain and fear.

"Watch for bushwhackers, Kurt. Let's take their weapons. We'll grab one of their horses to carry them."

"Alright, Shorty. What about the ones that are alive?"

"If they reach for a gun, shoot. Otherwise, let the varmints deal with their own hurt."

The two Wet Springs fighters gathered weapons. There were seven dead outlaws and three wounded. The one who had been crying bled out. Shorty tried to question a wounded fellow who was hit in the side and going fast.

"Willing to talk?" asked Shorty.

"Go to Hades."

"Maybe someday, but you first."

Kurt and Shorty stacked the arsenal on the ground. They captured several saddled horses with rifles and saddlebags. Shorty had Kurt keep the horses and effects.

"Let's go," said the older man.

After a while, Shorty asked Kurt a question.

"Do you get nervous when you're in a shooting scrape?"

"No, but my blood does get up a bit."

"Haw, haw, mine too. Just wonderin. What made you jump down and start shooting like that?"

"I saw they figured out who we were. There were too many. We had surprise on our side. Who can hit anything from a riled horse?"

"Son, you're one to ride the river with."

"Shorty, don't call me son. Call me by my rightful name."

"Kurt, you have my word on it for as long as I live."

Coming close to the ranch, they heard gunfire. Apparently another group was attacking the house. Kurt and Shorty stopped their horses and listened."

"What now?" asked Kurt.

"You seem to be better at this than me, what do you suggest?"

"I'd hide the horses, get the extra rifles, rig some way to carry them along with ammunition, food, and canteens."

"Then what?"

"There's that peak overlooking the ranch. Let's climb that and provide cover."

"Who taught you this stuff, Kurt?"

"You did.

"You're going to have me swelled up like a toad. Hurry, let's get to the doing."

Heavy barrages of fire would occur, then a series of single shots. It sounded like a war. From the direction of the ranch house, they could hear a number of shots as well. Every once in a while one of those .50 caliber Sharps would sound.

"Kurt, too bad we don't have one of those .50's with the scope. We've got all these rifles, but they won't shoot very far."

"We have to try to do something."

"Sure, son, I mean, Kurt. We'll do what we can."

They found a set of deep saddlebags and loaded the rifles, butt first, into each side. Shorty was to carry this.

Kurt took another set of saddlebags and filled each side with canteens, some jerky, some canned peaches he found, and ammunition. They hid the horses on a grassy slope, in the shade next to the high peak, and began to climb. This was a place where Kurt had played a thousand times. There were two ways up and down. Kurt led Shorty up the most direct route. They were both panting when they came to the top. They lay low and looked down.

They could see the large barn with its red-tiled roof, the corral behind the stable, the horses, the chicken coop, and little dots of hens running around. They saw the pig shelter with its large adobe wall and the pigs inside. They saw the wooden bunkhouse that was built for the Mexican workers. There was the red-tiled adobe building that was for Charlie, Dan, and Shorty, Carlos and Juan's cabin, and the big ranch house.

The view from the cliff was spectacular. This was an angle of the ranch that Shorty had never seen before. How picturesque and pristine it looked. What he saw below was the creation from the vivid mind of Priscilla West. The scene gave no indication of the blood, sweat, and tears that had gone into it.

The only signs of struggle from this distance were the white puffs of smoke discharging from the shuttered windows of the ranch house. They could see someone on top of the parapet of the house aim and fire, and then disappear as they crouched low. To the southeast was a group of horses and some men gathered around a fire. By concentrating they could see little dots of men off to the east. The closest view of the attacking outlaws was to the north. A few men were firing at the ranch house. This was maybe five hundred yards away. Further back was another group of men and horses with a campfire going. Poindexter had planned a siege.

"What do we do now?" asked Kurt.

"If I had a Sharps, I could nail those men to the north."

"We don't have one. Besides, it's only a single shooter. They would hide in the rocks after the first couple shots."

"Alright, what do you suggest?"

"Stay here through the night and see what happens. Maybe they'll try to hit the house tonight, and if the moon's out, we'll be able to shoot. If there is no change tomorrow, we can join those at the ranch."

"Sounds like as good a plan as any. You know, it's gets awfully cold up here at night."

"I'll run back to the horses and grab a couple of the outlaws' bedding. Be right back."

"Be careful."

Shorty lay at the edge of the cliff and looked out over the ranch. How deceptively tranquil it looked. Time dragged on. The white puffs and then the discharge of a weapon would reverberate and make its way to Shorty's ears.

Maybe I should go back and find Poindexter and just kill him, he thought. *"Doesn't matter what happens to me. That's the only real way to end this. Why would God create someone like the Wests, Kurt, my pards, or that priest, and then make someone like Poindexter? Don't make no sense."*

The sun on the rocks and Shorty's back was hot. The sky was its usual pristine blue with a cloud here and there.

Shorty flipped over and tried to look up toward the sun and could not. He sneezed. A Red-tailed hawk sailed by and squealed its haunting cry. Shorty reached for a saddlebag, took out a canteen, and drank.

Good God, he sighed, and then looked up at a white fleecy cloud slowly changing shape. *How good it is to be alive. To breathe air, to swallow a cool drink of water, to smell, to hear, to see. Such simple pleasures. How wonderful to feel the warm sun. Why then all this guilt? Cause I'm still alive and my pards are in the ground? Could they be in Heaven? Sure sounded like it when Father Torres talked. Now there is a man.*

Shorty looked around. A lot of time had gone by and no Kurt. Another few minutes and he would go look for him.

Now, how about that Kurt? Shorty continued thinking to himself. *He is already one of the great ones. What brainpower, what nerve, what maturity. He was born a man, his body just had to catch up with him. It's his nerve that makes him different. When he was a youngster he wanted to save his dad, so he did. He set out to save the filly and the kitten, and he did that too. His father and mother needed a gunfighter, and he became one. Age is not a factor with this boy."*

"What are you mumbling?" asked Kurt as he came up behind Shorty and set four bedrolls down.

"Nothin," Shorty smiled. "Just con-tem-pla-tin. Me and myself was havin' a little conversation. You unroll them blankets and check 'em out. I hate fleas. I'd rather freeze to death than get fleas. I'm allergic to the darn things. Swell up like a sausage."

"Alright baby," said Kurt. "Be like the princess and the pea, all delicate like."

"Here, give me two, I'll check em out myself."

They lay up there through the day and into the night. Kurt had carried up some beans, corn, peaches, and jerky. One of the outlaws had a bottle of whiskey. Shorty took it and had a long pull and then corked it and put it on his bedroll. They sat and chewed on jerky, ate the vegetables and finished them off with succulent peaches. Sporadic gunfire continued down below, and there was nothing they could do about it.

They watched until after ten o'clock at night. Kurt fell asleep. Shorty himself had trouble keeping awake. He would guard until two o'clock and would ask the boy to finish the watch. Standing up, his thoughts eventually won out over sleepiness. He sat on a rock and watched a full moon rise. It shone bright and created dark shadows. What they call a hunters moon, with enough light to shoot by.

It was after midnight when Shorty could see men from three sides start to move towards the house. Shorty nudged Kurt and got no response. The older man gave up and threw cold water on the boy's face. Kurt came awake gasping and sat up. Shorty put a hand over the young man's mouth and pointed down. Then he gave the youth one of the rifles.

The moon was up, and the stars shone like diamonds against the black of the sky. It was almost as bright as day. Shorty and Kurt watched the men. Some of them were carrying a ladder. It appeared they were going to try to climb onto the parapet. Others were heading towards the house, where they could stick their guns into the ports.

Maybe they even had dynamite.

No one from the house saw them coming. Perhaps the guard was sleeping. There were more than twenty men advancing. Shorty waited until they were right near the house, then he aimed and fired. The distance was several hundred yards. A man fell. Kurt started shooting, aiming and firing as fast as he could lever shells into the Winchester. Shorty did the same. The man and boy used rifle after rifle, emptying them and moving onto the next. They shot accurately and with so many loaded weapons to use, their firepower was as if a small army was atop the mountain. Dead and wounded lay on the ground next to the house. The occupants wakened and contributed to the death toll. They were sending out a heavy barrage of fire. The remaining outlaws dropped everything—rifles, ladder, hats—in their effort to run as fast as their feet would take them. It was funny, in a deadly sort of way.

"Don't laugh, Kurt, shoot the murderin' coyotes. Don't stop firing until they're somewhere hot."

They both kept shooting from their high position and didn't stop until their rifles were empty. Towards the last, they were elevating them and trying to lob shots down on the fleeing raiders. Poindexter's men kept right on running straight to their horses, and those that lived galloped away. It was an image that the two Wet Springs men would never forget.

Shorty and Kurt hurriedly gathered up the weapons and saddlebags and headed down, leaving bedrolls. They walked back to the thirsty horses and mounted and rode towards the house. Kurt yelled in a high clear voice to open the door for Shorty and him. John and Priscilla ran out and hugged them. Issy and Juan took the horses to the corral behind the house to unsaddle, water, and feed. After several minutes of excited talk, Shorty and Kurt said they were exhausted and needed to go to bed. Time enough in the morning to swap stories.

John and Priscilla took the load of guns into the house. Shorty warned everyone that there could still be snipers out there and that in the morning things could start up again. They knew this was probably true and agreed to use the tunnels to come in for breakfast.

Shorty went to the adobe bunkhouse and opened the door. He stood in the quiet of the room and looked around in the dark. The thought of Charlie and Dan was too great. The pain created by the memory of the rooms was too much to endure.

"I can't sleep here."

He walked off to the log bunkhouse built for the workers, went in, picked a bunk, and collapsed on it. He was asleep within a few minutes.

Kurt went to the barn and straight to his room. Cindy ran to Kurt's window and whinnied softly. Opening the window, he laughed and pushed the mare away. Little Tiger meowed and tried to claw his way up Kurt's pant leg. He reached down and picked up the cat and petted him.

"Go to bed, you two, I'm too tired to play."

Kurt pulled off his boots and flopped down fully dressed.

After Issy and Juan had removed the saddles, saddlebags, and personal effects from the horses, they forked hay and made sure there was water in the trough. They harnessed two draft horses to one of the wagons. They drove around the grounds picking up bodies, loading them into the back of the wagon. When finished, they dumped the dead in an arroyo. They stomped from above, and walls of loose earth fell down and covered the bodies. With the next heavy rain, the dry wash would quickly flood, and these dozen or so men would be washed miles away and out onto the dry plain.

In the morning Kurt was awakened by his pets. The racket of pounding hoofs and whinnying was a bit disconcerting. Little Tiger stood on Kurt's chest and was licking the underside of his neck. Kurt got up and forked hay for Cindy and fixed food for his cat. He washed up and changed his clothes. Preparing for what might come next, he went to a side section of the large barn, pulled on a rope, and the wooden floor lifted, exposing a stairway. He took a lantern that was hanging there, lit it, and descended. Kurt pulled on another rope; the floor came down and closed behind him. He followed the tunnel to the main house.

The sun was up when Shorty awoke. He was groggy and still tired and needed to clean up and change clothes. The only place to do that was back in his room. What the devil was he doing in this log cabin? It was daylight out, and there was no tunnel under this building. He could get shot walking around out there.

Shorty opened the door cautiously, it seemed quiet. He started around the log building toward his adobe house.

Then he felt something tear at his leg and down he went. A shot echoed and Shorty realized someone was shooting at him. He got up and hopped as fast as he could. Bullets careened around him. He made it to the door of the adobe bunkhouse, opened it, relieved to find shelter.

Shorty looked at his left leg. He cursed. He pulled up on his torn pant leg and saw a red groove with part of his shinbone exposed. The little man swore some more. Gritting his teeth against the pain, he went in his bedroom and tightened a belt above the wound to stop the bleeding. He then took off the Mexican clothes he was still wearing and quickly washed. The pain was making him sick as he hurriedly dressed. He entered the common room of the adobe and went to a table. He lifted it, and a portion of the floor came with it. Underneath was a built-in ladder leading to the tunnel. Shorty went down and lit a lantern. He limped along the tunnel to the ranch house.

The darn polecats won't leave us alone, he grunted. *Gosh, does my shin hurt. How many of them do we have to kill? Mrs. West sure was thinking when she had us build these tunnels and adobe buildings. Smart bosses I have.*

Shorty came up the ladder that opened into the living room of the ranch house. A part of the tiled floor was removed and then put back in place. The West crew was in the kitchen, eating, talking, and waiting for Shorty. Priscilla took one look at him and went for bandages, alcohol, and laudanum. Shorty sat down and Priscilla examined him.

"Good luck and bad, Shorty," she told him.

"Why?"

"The good luck is you're alive. The bad is that this

wound, with a part of your bone missing, is going to hurt like heck and take a long time to heal."

"It figures. Hey Boss, have you got something I can take?"

"Drink this. It'll make you woozy, but it'll lessen the pain. Just don't ride any horses."

Shorty drank the dark-colored liquid, and within a few minutes, he wasn't feeling much of anything. In fact, to him, everything seemed just fine.

John, Priscilla, and the rest of Wet Springs crew sat at the large table and listened to Kurt's long explanation of the things that he and Shorty went through. Kurt told of the beautiful funeral, of the gunfight, of collecting weapons, and climbing to the high rock on the west side of the ranch. He explained how, from above, they stopped the late-night attack on the ranch house. Kurt went on to tell his parents that he talked to Father Torres about selling cattle to Spanish vaqueros. Father Torres had agreed to find buyers. Kurt explained that he asked for no less than fifteen dollars a head. He asked if he did right. John shook his son's hand, and his mother hugged him. Shorty was over in the corner staring at the designs in the floor tile.

CHAPTER ELEVEN

Two of Father Torres's assistants came to him in his private chambers and informed him that a man, a very dirty, smelly, wounded gringo, was lying in one of the pews in the back of the church. Father Torres followed and made his way to the large open sanctuary. The man was indeed filthy, blood was on his arm and side, and he did smell. Fear was evident in the man's eyes and his presence in the church meant he was seeking sanctuary. Painfully the man attempted to sit up.

"Father, I am asking for asylum. They're after me. This is the only safe place I could find. They're searching the buildings, and soon they will come here. Please hide me."

"What is your name?"

"Father, I have gone by a lot of names. Lately, I've been called Whiskey on account of my strong leaning for the stuff."

"You must explain more," said Father Torres firmly. "You endanger my people by your presence. What is your Christian name?"

"Zach, Father. Zachery Lemcool."

"Zachery, why should I endanger my church and my

people to help a man who worked for Poindexter? You have been an outlaw, a gunman, a bandit. Have you not?"

"You know?"

"You waste our time. Throw him out!" Father Torres ordered.

"No, you can't. They'll kill me."

"They will kill us and destroy the church if you are found here. Why should we take this risk?"

"I'll change. I'll turn over a new leaf. Please, Father."

"Answer this. You have been a gun for hire for a long time?"

"Yes, Father, but I never shot no one in the back. That's not so with most of Poindexter's men. Many are backshooters."

"Quickly, tell me one honest thing that may persuade me. Think hard, your life depends on it."

"What can I say? I regret many things. Whiskey's my problem. I wasn't raised this way. My mother brought me up in the church. I'll change, Father. I swear it."

"I need more than that, Zachery. I need your promise on the Holy Bible."

Father Torres took a small Bible from his robes and held it out.

"Place your hand here and swear, or leave."

Zachery put out a shaky, dirty hand. Father Torres grasped it and pushed down hard and with tremendous strength.

"Swear!"

"I swear, Father, to change my ways."

"As God and I are witnesses, you will keep this

promise."

Father Torres spoke in Spanish, and the two assistants helped the stranger up the aisle and to the rear chambers. A table and carpet were moved, and a trapdoor was pulled up, revealing stairs. The two helped the wounded man down and took him to a portion of a wall covered by a blanket. The wall moved and opened into another room. Inside were several beds, a table, and chairs. A lantern illuminated a water pitcher and basin. The two men went out and closed the secret door.

Zachery lay down on a bed. Within a few minutes, the wall opened again, and a very old woman entered. Behind her were the two men. The men set down several buckets and a bundle that contained soap, washcloth, towels, and clean clothes. The old woman laid an assortment of bandages and medicines out on the table.

With no-nonsense, the woman began to cut away Zachery's clothes. The wounded man complained.

"Don't be a fool," snapped the old woman in English. "Your wounds stink. Maybe gangrene starts. Now lay down and don't move."

Zachery did as he was told. She stripped him and covered him with a clean towel. He was washed thoroughly. The woman inspected the wound in his side and the more severe one in his shoulder. Both had seen no attention for days and were badly infected. The wound in the upper shoulder smelled.

She cleaned the bullet holes and scraped on them. Zachery sweated fiercely and groaned. She applied various medicines, a poultice, and tied a bandage around his middle to hold it in place. The wound in the shoulder was worse. Zachery was not sure what the old lady did because somewhere along the way he passed out. He thought before he went under that he smelled gunpowder and sulfur.

When Zachery awoke, Father Torres was sitting on a chair next to his bed reading.

"Ah, you look much better in those clean clothes. The smell of rotten flesh is gone. How do you feel, Señor Zachery?"

"Starved."

"A very good sign. Here is nourishment. You may eat."

Zachery tried to sit up, but dizziness overcame him. Father Torres helped place pillows behind his back. The priest took up a spoon and began feeding warm soup to the wounded man. Zachery swallowed hungrily. He had been hiding out on the streets of the town for several days without sustenance. Father Torres helped hold up a glass of water and Zachery gulped it down.

"Slowly," said the priest, "too fast and your stomach will protest."

Soon after, Zachery's body told him it craved alcohol, and he began to sweat. Father Torres noticed.

"If you have been drinking for years, you will go through much pain before your body changes. I have seen this before. Two good things—we have you hidden and locked in. We will not let you out until your need for drink subsides."

"Thank you, Father," whispered Zachery. "I pray I can do this."

There is more. The old woman who worked on your

wounds said another day, and she would have had to cut your arm off. Even that may not have saved you. God was merciful."

Zachery wiped his mouth and looked at his deliverer. "Thank you, Father, for helping me. I want to keep my promises, but I am not sure..."

"You are already on your way."

"I hope that is true, Father. I really do."

"In two weeks you will be much improved. I have a mission for you. I will tell you of it when the time is right. There is something I would ask. Were any of those dead men in the wagon friends of yours?"

"One of the wounded and one of the dead men were my pards; we were together a number of years."

"Then know this. Poindexter let the two wounded men, the dead bodies, and the horses attached to the wagon sit in the hot sun. The two men died. Complaints came, and Poindexter ordered two of his men to take the wagon south of town. The bodies were thrown out onto the open prairie. This is how Poindexter cares for his men."

"Father, I will do my best to keep my oath. But when I am better, I will go after that man."

"No, Señor Zachery, not alone. God put you into my hands, and I know a better way."

"Tell me."

"First, stay and heal. Your body has learned to crave drink, but it is your mind that has made it so. Your coming to us has put you on a new path. I will send you where you can begin to keep your promises."

CHAPTER TWELVE

Two and a half weeks later at Wet Springs Ranch, an owl began to hoot. A rather badly hooting owl at that. Kurt jumped up and ran to the patio door.

"Don't worry," said Kurt. "That's Father Torres's signal. It means we have an answer about our cattle."

The Wet Springs crew were in the ranch house where they had spent most of their time since the last raid. During the day they were fired upon by snipers. None of the outside ranch work was getting done. For target practice, some of the sharpshooters had shot a number of pigs. If it weren't for the tunnels and stored food, they probably wouldn't have survived. Something was going to have to be done to get the marksmen off the cliffs. The Wests didn't know it, but the answer to their problems would start with the knocking at their door.

Kurt answered it with his pistol drawn. He saw one Mexican wearing a large sombrero, and striped pants come to the patio and stop.

"I come from Father Torres, and I bring a message."

Kurt let him in and took the paper he held out. Not taking his eyes off the Mexican, Kurt gave the paper to his mother to read. The stranger stood quietly. He left his sombrero on. Priscilla read the note.

"It says that a group of vaqueros will come to the ranch within the week. They will arrive at midnight to purchase cattle and gather them for a drive. They will be expecting trouble and will be prepared to deal with it. Kurt, Father Torres says they will pay fifteen dollars a head! That's $3000.00 for our two hundred!"

"Good going, son," said Kurt's father.

"Wait, there is more. Father Torres states he has sent a man, Zachery, who will work for us. He says we will understand what he means."

The visitor before them took his hat off and Shorty jumped.

"The man with the wounded shoulder! He's one of Poindexter's!"

"Not anymore. Because I talked, Poindexter wants my life. Father Torres took me in when no one else would. He saved me."

"And…we're supposed to believe that?" shouted Shorty.

"He made me swear on a Bible."

"We should risk our lives and trust you for that?" said John West.

"Father said that if you didn't believe, to tell you this— Poindexter let the dead men in the wagon lie all day in the sun. The two wounded that you doctored, he let die. Two of those men on that wagon were my pards."

"How are we to believe any of this?" snarled Shorty.

"If you do not want me, I am to go back. But let me tell

you that I also hate Poindexter for what he did. At dusk he had his men take the wagon out of town and dump the bodies on the ground. Father Torres sent me to help you, and I will do it if you let me."

"I believe him," said Kurt. "If Father Torres trusts him, so do I."

"I agree," responded John. "What do you think, Priscilla?"

"I don't believe we have any other choice but to hire him and see how he does."

"Then it's settled," said John. "Shorty, I want you to take Zachery under your wing and work with him. Give him one of the rooms." John hesitated, then gripped Shorty's arm. "Shorty, no matter how much it galls you, do it. You owe a debt to the good priest, remember?"

"Can't you get someone else?"

"Shorty, you're indispensable. We don't have the luxury to throw away hands."

"If you say so."

"Zachery," said John, "will you have a problem taking orders from Carlos and Juan?"

"No, sir, Mr. West. It was a group of Mexicans who doctored me, fed me, and saved my life."

"Good." John shook hands.

A week later, in the middle of the night, the thundering of hooves was heard. The Wests were waiting and prepared. Vaqueros rode up to the patio and dismounted. Dust was everywhere. Smartly dressed Mexican's stood holding their horses. The saddles and trappings were intricately worked; the tack was decorated with silver. The horses themselves were exquisite.

"I come to talk to Señor and Señora West," said the leader of the group. "I am Antoya Valdez. This is the Wet Springs Ranch, is it not?"

"It is and welcome. I'm John West, and this is my wife, Priscilla. Come inside. The rest of you, please make yourselves comfortable. We will bring food and refreshment."

Carlos stood beside John, ready to translate if necessary. Inside the house, Kurt and Issy helped Priscilla prepare the repast. In the kitchen, Carmen and Rosa poured cool drinks and put food on large platters for their guests. Tables and chairs were set up on the patio, and Kurt and Issy took plates, cups, knives, and forks out and set them on tables. Then they carried out large trays heavily laden with meats and cheese and fresh bread.

"This is very gracious of you to serve my men."

"You are doing us a great service," said John. "Feeding you is the least we can do. After all, we were able to prepare; we knew you were coming. We are honored that you are our guests. I am sorry it has to be in the middle of the night. You see, by day we are shot at from the cliffs. They are cowards and shoot to kill from a distance. Still, no matter how many we eliminate, over the years, they keep coming."

"In this life, Señor West, one's enemies take on many forms, and they always keep on coming. Why don't you send someone into the hills to find these snipers?"

"Mainly, Antoya, because we don't have enough men.

We have already had too many killed. Many of us have been wounded, and unfortunately, we play this game against superior odds. We have no idea the outcome, but we keep running the ranch as best we can."

"We were told to come prepared to fight banditos," said Valdez. "We must clear out this nest of vipers to get at the cattle, is that not so?"

"Yes."

"Then we shall do it. I have brought three Yaqui Indians. With three more of my men, they will go into the hills and find these shooters. I would not want to be one of these bad men. Tomorrow these banditos will find it most difficult to breathe. Their deaths will be silent ones. The Yaqui's are good trackers and shall we say, very good with cold steel."

"Now, thar's the way it should be done," shouted Jedidiah.

"We take in the old, the lame, and the feebleminded," John laughed.

"Hey thar, young man!"

"Shut up, Jedidiah," said Shorty. "Can't you see they are palavering about important stuff?"

"I see your men are as interesting and unusual as mine," smiled Valdez. "One more question before I partake of this fine meal. How long do you believe it will take for us to gather the cattle?"

"Assuming the snipers are gone?"

"Oh, I assure you, they will be eliminated."

"That being the case, gathering them will be easy. The cattle are penned up in a canyon. They have overgrazed and are ready to be moved out. You should be able to herd them quickly. You can take count at the gate. We will leave a few for breeding stock."

"Very good, Señor West. We go get the heard in the morning and after the count, we will finish the money business. No offense, but I do not wish to expose my men to further trouble."

"No offense taken."

They ate, and the talk was friendly. Antoya Valdez got up and said it was late, and sleep for his men was essential. He and several of his vaqueros were offered beds in the house, but he declined. On the patio, tables and chairs were moved, and the men brought their bedrolls and laid them out. Their horses were unsaddled, and some were put in the stables and others in the corral. Issy and Kurt helped with the extra water and feed.

Early in the morning, before sunrise, six dark shapes made their way into the mountain rocks. Towards dawn, animals living in the mountains heard stifled screams and strange sounds.

A couple hours after daybreak, Valdez woke the rest of his men. He had deliberately let them sleep late. Breakfast and gallons of coffee had already been prepared by Priscilla, Carmen, and Rosa. Some of the vaqueros attempted to flirt with the women. Valdez promptly put an end to this. The men ate hungrily—some sitting and others standing. When they were finished, they politely thanked their hosts.

The Spanish speaking cattlemen headed out to the corrals and stables in search of their horses and saddles. Their gear was stacked together in the barn. Carlos, John, Issy, and Kurt were there to help. Shorty stood off some distance. He was very nervous about the snipers.

Horses caught and saddled, the heavily armed vaqueros mounted and rode for the canyon. It was a colorful yet deadly looking group of riders. With confidence, they rode in the open. The Wet Springs crew joined them.

Far up on the cliff, Shorty saw a man rise up with a rifle in his hands. What looked like an Indian hopped up on a rock nearby, took a running jump through the air, and landed behind the man. Before the rifleman could turn, a flash of light shone on a large blade, and the Indian swiped at the cowboy's neck. A flood of crimson flowed. The body, along with his rifle, fell over the cliff and dropped onto the rocks below.

With so many vaqueros gathering cattle and doing it much better than any of the Wet Springs crew could, John let them alone. As they came through the gate, Shorty and a couple of vaqueros counted. Shorty got 203, the vaqueros 201. John let it go at that. Valdez came up and paid John with sacks of gold.

"It is all there, Señor West, three thousand. Count it if you like."

"No, Señor Valdez. Trust is a mutual thing. You have done Wet Springs Ranch a valuable service. You and your men are welcome as our guests anytime."

"Thank you, Señor West. You have been very gracious. Great success to you with your war against these bad hombres. Via con Dios."

The trained horses of the vaqueros moved the steers effortlessly, and they headed south and off the ranch. The dust from the herd sent up a great cloud that probably could be seen a far distance. Yet, there was no one who came to chase the herd, and there were no snipers shooting from the cliffs.

CHAPTER THIRTEEN

After Valdez and his vaqueros took away the herd, nearly two years passed with no further trouble. Priscilla often commented to John that it felt like the lull before the storm. Kurt and Issy, more like two brothers than friends, took a greater part in the responsibility of running the ranch. They had taken the mares that were found among the confiscated horses and released them into the canyon for breeding stock. Besides guns, the outlaws also knew horses, and their mounts were excellent horseflesh. Kurt and Issy also took two stallions, offspring from the thoroughbred mare, and released them in the canyon. Issy and Kurt anticipated great results. They were sure of foals of exceptional merit.

Lessons continued for the young men at the big kitchen table. Both were good scholars.

Issy and Kurt had taken to riding around the ranch and checking out the cliffs and hidden places. They sometimes found partial skeletons, pistols, knives, and rifles— evidence left by the dead outlaws that were killed in the fighting. One particular place they found was a horse trail that led up a cliff and then stopped on the rise. The trail continued on down the other side and to the east. What was interesting was that one could tie a horse off where there was a little grass, and then on foot take an ancient trail up to the top of a cliff. This was, without a doubt, the highest promontory on all of Wet Springs Ranch and the view, whether day or night, was magnificent.

One day Kurt and Issy went to what they now referred to as Promontory Point. They rode up, and there was another horse there! The horse had a Poindexter brand! The young men climbed the trail cautiously, pistols drawn. When they reached the top, both breathing hard and hearts pounding, they stopped in amazement.An attractive, longhaired girl sat demurely on a rock and stared back at them. She had amazing green eyes.

Kurt and Penelope together
at Promontory Point

"Are you going to shoot me or stare me to death?" asked Penelope Poindexter.

"What are you doing here?" asked Kurt.

"Isn't it obvious? I came to see you."

"Why?"

"Because I was lonely and bored, and mostly to meet the boy who stood up to my horrible stepfather. Is that reason enough?"

"It wasn't me alone. It was Poindexter who forced our hand. Nothing more."

"They call you Kid Kurt, the boy gunfighter."

Despite the flattery, Kurt bristled.

"That was two years ago, and I am not a boy!"

"Why quibble? Who is your friend?"

"Penelope, this is Issy, my good friend who lives at Wet Springs. Issy, this is Penelope—the girl we have talked about—Poindexter's stepdaughter."

"It is a very great pleasure to meet you, Señorita Penelope."

"Issy," said the girl rising and shaking hands.

"Enough. Really, Penelope, why do you risk coming here?"

"Is it a risk?"

"You know it is. If one of your stepfather's men find you out riding alone, who knows what might happen to you."

"They wouldn't dare touch me."

"Any decent man, no, but your stepfather doesn't hire decent men."

"I have this. My mother gave it to me."

She drew a shiny nickel-plated pistol from a leather pocket of her skirt.

"Do you know how to shoot it?"

She aimed and shot Kurt's sombrero off his head.

"Very funny. Where did you learn?"

"From an old hand, a friend of my mother's. This is the only thing that protects me from my stepfather. He has been after me for years. He knows I would shoot him if he touched me."

"Why don't you and your mother leave him?"

"I would instantly, but mother..." She let this trail off. "He has some hold on her. I don't know what it is."

"That's too bad."

"He's like a snake mesmerizing its prey. I loathe him. I would leave in a minute but for Mother. Do you understand?"

"No."

"Let's change the subject. Come, Issy and Kurt," said Penelope patting the rock on each side of her. "Let's sit and eat our picnic."

Kurt and Issy exchanged wondering glances.

Penelope reached in front of a large stone and pulled up a basket. She took out plates, cloth napkins, little sandwiches, chicken, and a large bottle of still cold sarsaparilla. She poured the sparkling liquid into cups and handed them to her companions.

"I just love sarsaparilla, don't you?"

They spent the rest of the afternoon together. Kurt talked of the outlaws who had sat in the rocks and shot at them. They spoke of exploring the mountain cliffs trying to find hiding places and more pistols and rifles. They talked of their studies, the wonderful stories by Mark Twain, and their futures. The three of them discussed their isolation and how it would be wonderful to have parties or fiestas. They imagined how great it would be if Poindexter disappeared and all the conflict stopped. They agreed to meet again each Wednesday on the promontory. She said there might be times she would not be able to get away but promised she would try.

Issy and Kurt said nothing of the meeting with Penelope. They decided to keep it a secret and went about their business. They were given more chores around the stable. Both begged for help and more hands to feed the pigs, chickens, and horses, and to take care of shoveling the mountains of manure. Kurt's father referred to it as dark gold. Laying the smelly stuff out on the fields would result in greater yields of grass. The boys continued their complaint, and Father Torres was contacted about finding more ranch hands.

When the fighting had stopped, Father Torres began to visit the ranch more often. He came out several times a month. Now when he came, it was always with armed escorts. The last time he brought four more men with him to work for the Wests. The workers moved into the log bunkhouse.

The priest checked up on Zachery and was pleased to learn he was keeping his promises. Zachery, it turned out, was the son of a stonemason. John had him building dams and irrigation ditches. Zachery was also a fair hand at cattle and, like most cowboys, was a jack of all trades. Since Zachery had quit drinking, he had lost weight and the puffiness around his face and belly. The man was regaining his health and dignity. He liked working for the Wests.

Old man Jedidiah Taylor was the real thorn in the flesh for the residents at Wet Springs. He was a talker, a nuisance, and somewhat of a moocher. On top of that, the old man smelled. Everyone complained, but Priscilla reminded them of the promise two years ago when he stood up for them in front of the townspeople and Poindexter.

"I said he had a home with us, and that is a promise I will not allow to be broken," she said adamantly."

The day was hot; tempers were hotter. Shorty came into the large cabin—angry, tired, and fighting mad. "Boss, those darn bulls have knocked down that north canyon gate again. We have to round up half the herd."

Old Jedidiah stepped in just behind Shorty. "What you so riled up about, Shorty? Ain't got no sweet señorita to come close to you lately?" he teased.

Shorty exploded. "Shut up, you stinkin old coot. Nobody on this ranch can get close to you—never could. You stink worse than a manure pile that's been left sittin in the sun for a week. Go take a bath and give us some air. Sure was a lot better around here before you showed up to stink us out."

Old man Jedidiah stopped short, "If I ain't welcome around here, I'll go. Mrs. West, is that how it is?"

Priscilla put her hand on the old man's broad shoulder. "Jedidiah, of course you have a home with us. But, there are some things we need to talk about. I am sorry, I should have sooner."

"Mrs. West," Jedidiah's voice quivered. "Don't you go beating around no bush. You got somethin' to say to me, then say it."

"Jedidiah," said Priscilla. "I have been getting a lot of complaints, and I have to talk to you."

"About what?"

"About a lot of things."

"I've got a tough hide, ma'am; I reckon I can take it."

"I'm concerned about your health. Carmen, Rosa, and I need to fix you up. We want you to move out of that shed and into the bunkhouse with Shorty and Zachery. But, before you can do that, we want you to clean up and stay clean. You're too old to sleep in that old shed. The adobe bunkhouse is heated. You would have your own room and bed."

"If you say so."

"That's not all. It's not healthy for you to wear the same clothes and not wash them. And it's not right for you to sit around all day. You need to find something to do."

"Like what?"

"You think about it, but for right now, we need to get you cleaned up."

"Are you saying I need a bath?"

"Yes, Jedidiah."

"Why didn't you say so in the first place? My sniffer don't work so well. Ever since some Ute tonked me on the head. That was years ago."

"We want to give you some clothes, enough to change and wash every other day."

"I'm thinkin I could guard the ranch. Can you give me one of those fancy Sharps with the scope? My eyes aren't what they use to be."

"Only if you promise to wash up every few days and change into clean clothes. You don't do that, and no one here at Wet Spring is going to be happy with you."

"I smell pretty bad, do I?"

"Awful," Priscilla confessed, wrinkling her nose.

"Why didn't somebody tell me? Say, can I have a saddle, saddlebags, a horse—the works?"

"You sit and take a bath, let me cut your hair, and you've got yourself a deal. And you think about what you can do for us. Something to keep you busy."

"Can I shoot outlaws?"

"I don't know. You would have to talk to John about that."

"Alright, ma'am. Old Jedidiah will change his ways. You been powerful good to me. I don't know if you noticed, but I've been filling out and gettin stronger."

Priscilla, Carmen, and Rosa brought water and filled a tin bathtub out on the patio. They added hot water, and then John and Carlos held up a blanket while the old-timer stripped. He dropped his filthy, rank clothes, and stepped into the tub. While he was making a big ceremony about being wet all over, and complaining that taking a bath was plain unhealthy, John and Carlos got a look at the old man's body. His pale white skin was covered with old wounds and scars. Some looked like bullet wounds, some arrow holes, and several knife wounds. Apparently the stories he told weren't so farfetched. There was more to this old man than met the eye.

Carlos picked up the dirty clothes, underwear, boots, and hat with a stick and put them in a wheelbarrow for Kurt and Issy to take and burn. The old man sat in the tub sputtering about not wanting no woman seeing him without his boots on. Together, Priscilla and Carmen gave John copious amounts of soap and perfumes for the bathwater. John and Carlos took turns scrubbing the old man with a brush. He didn't like it one bit. They washed his hair several times with strong soap. The water was black.

With the old man hollering about catching his death of cold, they pulled the plug on the washtub and let the water run out. They added cold and hot water as quickly as they could. Jedidiah shouted bloody murder. Finally, they added enough warm water for him to shut up, it turned just as black. Jedidiah's skin was cleaner, and he looked several shades lighter.

They again pulled the plug and drained the water. As Jedidiah stood, John handed him a clean towel to dry with. The towel was white, and parts of it turned black when the oldster wiped his body and dried his hair. John gave Jedidiah another towel to wrap around his waist and then pushed him into the house. Together, John and Carlos guided the old man into the kitchen.

Priscilla came with a medical bag and set it down on the table beside him. She told Jedidiah to be quiet and reminded him that he had promised to do this. Just as soon as he put on new clothes, he could get the rifle, saddle, horse, and whatever else he needed. That shut him up.

Priscilla examined the old man's chest and arms. She asked where the scars came from and she had to cut him off from launching into long explanations. She shortened it to a yes or no, by pointing and asking if his scar was a knife, gun, or arrow wound? She examined his legs and feet. He had good flesh tone and a lot of hard muscle from years of outdoor life. She had him turn over, and she immediately found a hard lump in the old man's back. She pushed on the lump, and when the old man jumped, she stopped.

Then she ordered Kurt and Issy to ride for Doctor Bennett.

Priscilla checked his heart, and it seemed sound. This was one tough old man who would probably live a long time. She checked his teeth. Most were in good shape; some would have to come out. She would ask Dr. Bennett to tend to that.

Jedidiah was given the items promised. With a new haircut, a clean face, and new clothes, he didn't look like the same man. He even walked with a firmer step. He looked in a large mirror that they brought him and the old man became quite emotional.

"Just nobody cared enough about me to do this. I sure am obliged. I'll treat you folks right from now on. That's my promise."

"Jedidiah," said Priscilla. "You sure look grand. I don't know what can be done for your back, but we're bringing out Dr. Bennett."

"Thank you, ma'am. It has been bothering me of late."

Dr. Bennett arrived at the ranch the next evening and stayed for several days. He took one look at Jedidiah and hardly recognized the same old mountain man he had seen around town. He examined him and was amazed at the transformation. Jedidiah didn't like it, but Dr. Bennett said he had to operate on his back.

In spite of the old man's protests, Dr. Bennett put him to sleep, and Priscilla assisted. First, he removed two rotten teeth and then tended to his back. The lump was cut open, broken bits of metal, and an old piece of arrowhead was removed. The doctor cleaned the wound and sewed it shut. He finished bandaging and gave Priscilla instructions on its care until it healed.

Later that evening, the Wests and the doctor went riding to the canyon. He was shown the gate, the cattle, the horses, the dams, the irrigation canals, and the growing fields of green grass. He was amazed at the amount of planning, forethought, and labor that had gone into the ranch. The doctor was delighted with the horse he was riding, and John and Priscilla gave it, the saddle, and bridle as a gift.

"Say," said the doctor, "I have nothing planned for the rest of the day. Can I stay and see your son and those animals I've heard so much about?"

"Why, of course," responded Priscilla.

Dr. Bennett shook hands with Kurt and was amazed to see the horse and cat follow the young man around as if he were their parent. The filly rubbed up against Kurt constantly and sought his attention. The cat did the same. The horse and cat would both lick him; the cat would jump up on the back of the filly, stand on his hind legs, and put his paws on Kurt's chest. The horse put up with the cat's claws in his back and, from time to time, the filly would lick the cat.

Kurt explained that he had to lock the animals in the stable, or they would get out and follow him. They could also follow his trail by sniffing it out, and they had found him miles from the ranch. When Dr. Bennett tried to pet the mare and cat they snarled and both bit at his hand.

Dr. Bennett sat on the patio drinking coffee with the Wests and explained that people in town were talking of their exploits with Poindexter and his gunslingers. He said that the most controversial story going round was how over forty men attacked Wet Springs Ranch and encountered fortifications instead of a rickety wooden ranch house. He said Poindexter's men talked of sharpshooters using large-caliber rifles.

"It seems after that fight," explained Dr. Bennett, "Poindexter had many of his men quit on him. Or rather, they just disappeared in the night. For a long while, the town noticed a change, especially on Saturday nights. There was less noise, less fighting, and far fewer assaults."

"I don't think we can take credit for that," commented Kurt.

"How many men did you fight that night? There's a legend about Wet Springs Ranch. That you are somehow protected."

"I bet Father Torres had something to do with that," said Priscilla.

"That's why Poindexter is having such a hard time hiring men. But I bet Poindexter is up to something. You folk's best be careful."

CHAPTER FOURTEEN

Dr. Bennett left Wet Springs Ranch, driving his buggy with the gift horse tied behind. "You can't find finer folks anywhere than the Wests," he mumbled to both horses. "There has to be a way to get Poindexter off their backs before more of them get killed."

Dr. Bennett paid the livery boy an extra quarter to unharness and rub-down the horses.

"Doc," said the young man taking the reins. "Mrs. Schmidt came by to see if your horse was here and asked if you might be about. Said she needed to see you about somethin'."

The dining room was empty except for Mrs. Schmidt, who sat in her usual seat near the kitchen door. She looked up from her writing as she heard footsteps.

"Why, Dr. Bennett, I have been hoping to talk with you today," she said, a serious expression on her face. "I have been worried sick. I heard you were called out to Wet Springs. Are the Wests alright? Did Poindexter and his men attack them again?"

The doctor reached out and patted her hand, "No, nothing like that. They just wanted me to take a look at old man Jedidiah. Seems there is more to him and his stories than meets the eye. No, the Wests are fine—for the moment at least. Sure do wish there was a way to help them against Poindexter."

"That's what I wanted to talk to you about," answered Mrs. Schmidt. "I have been working on some letters that might help. I want to know what you think of them." She looked cautiously around her and then slid the paper across the table to the doctor.

Dr. Bennett gave out a low whistle. "Do you realize what will happen to you if Poindexter finds out about this?" he asked. "A letter like this to the territorial governor might bring on some serious consequences—or—it might save our town, the Wests, and Wet Springs Ranch. Everything depends on whether the governor is in Poindexter's pocket. Are you willing to take that chance?"

Mrs. Schmidt's eyes blazed, "I thought you were their friend."

"Hold on. Of course I am their friend. I'm just asking if you have considered the consequences. This is not the first letter the governor will receive. I mailed a similar one just before I was called to Wet Springs. I implicated the judge, the sheriff, and other officials. In fact, Mrs. Schmidt, it may not be to your best interest to be seen with me in a few days—after the letter reaches the governor."

"I apologize," Mrs. Schmidt whispered contritely. "If I had known, we could have stood together in our efforts. I think there are many people who would be willing to stand with us if they knew we were united. The Wests have been good to our town—they didn't care if people were

Mexican or white or if they were rich or poor—they have treated everyone fairly. I think many of those people will stand up with us."

"I am certain you are right," agreed the doctor. "But they too have suffered greatly under Poindexter—even lost family members and their ranches. They are very frightened, and they have good reason to be."

"Dr. Bennett," answered Mrs. Schmidt sternly. "Don't you think I, of all people, know what Poindexter is capable of doing? He has threatened to burn our business if we allow Mexicans he has intimidated to purchase goods. And, I am ashamed to admit, Mr. Schmidt has often given in to Poindexter's demands. I refuse to sit by any longer and see innocent people and our friends persecuted like this without trying to do something. Will you work with me? Can we work together to try to get help? Not just for the Wests, but for our town? Even try to get the Federal Marshall to come and enforce the law?"

"By all means," grinned the doctor at the gutsy little lady. "By all means."

CHAPTER FIFTEEN

Father Torres, with several armed men, rode onto Wet Springs Ranch where they were warmly greeted. Shorty gave the priest a bear hug—quite new behavior for this diminutive gunfighter. It was the end of the day, and Zachery had just come in from cleaning up. Father Torres shook hands with his latest protégé. Due to his recent surgery, Jedidiah lay on a cot on the large veranda. He waved to the priest. Father Torres was amazed how changed the old man looked.

The women wasted no time preparing a delicious repast. They served food on the patio.

"Father, we are honored that you and your friends came to join us for dinner," said Priscilla graciously.

"Señora West, we are grateful for your generosity and hospitality. Food is so scarce in town that these men and I appreciate being invited to your home to eat."

"This sounds serious, Father. Tell us about it."

"Señor Poindexter has virtually eliminated work for my people; he threatens anyone who hires them. He has forced others to sell him their homes and land and then rents it back to them at rates they cannot afford. The stores charge my people more for food and clothing. Poindexter's men assault our women. They beat and kill our men. We are desperate now, and all of us fear for our lives."

Priscilla stood up, obviously angry.

"Father, why weren't we told of this before? Kurt, Issy, Juan, Carlos and Shorty," she ordered, "Go up to the canyon and bring down five steers. When the good priest leaves for town, you will help drive the cattle with him. You will take them where he directs you to have them butchered."

"We'll go right now, mother," said Kurt.

"John," said Priscilla, "if you will agree, bring the two money belts that Issy and Juan found on the night of the last raid. Rosa and Carmen, have one of the men bring a hundred-pound bag of salt out of the cellar—also, a hundred-pound bag of rice and another of flour."

John returned with the money belts.

"Father Torres, these money belts were found on two of the leaders who raided our ranch in the middle of the night," said John. "I think they came from Poindexter. We believe that the men were to be paid after the raid."

"We never counted it, Father," said Priscilla. "We considered it dirty money. We wondered what to do with it. You may take it for your people; that would be the right use for it."

"What a blessing that would be! May I count it?" asked Father Torres.

"We shall help you," said Priscilla.

Father Torres opened and dumped the contents of the money belt on the table. He counted out forty twenty-dollar gold pieces.

"That makes a total of eight hundred dollars," said the priest.

Priscilla opened the other one, and it had a name on it and appeared to be the owner's private belt. This one contained paper money, silver and gold coins. She counted a little over a thousand dollars.

With a tremor in his voice, the priest asked. "Would you truly give this to my people?"

"Yes, Father. After all, it is blood money."

"God works in mysterious ways. To think this, which was spent to cause you harm, will keep my people alive. God bless you. We will continue to pray for you and your kindness, my friends. We will not forget this gift."

"Father, you and your people have helped us many times," said Priscilla sincerely. "This is the very least we can do."

The Wet Springs crew rode guard while two of Father Torres's men drove one of the wagons containing the sacks of food. The priest was in a hurry to get back to town.

CHAPTER SIXTEEN

Improvement at Wet Springs Ranch was a way of life. Through the next couple of years, even more irrigation work was completed under John's leadership. He insisted that the water running out of the stream onto the dry ground below the ranch should be used. He built an irrigated corral.

Priscilla asked her husband to plant grass alongside the house. John refused and argued that a higher grass slope could not be irrigated.

"Why do you have to be such a mule-headed man, John West?" Priscilla argued. "It will keep the dust down, making it much less work to keep the house clean."

It was Zachery who finally came up with the solution. "Ma'am, what do you say we lay stones? That would work."

John and the rest of the men glared at Zachery.

"Do you realize what kind of job that will be?" complained John.

Priscilla was ecstatic.

"That's a better idea. Thank you, Zachery, you will be in charge."

The day they began to lay stones, had been particularly

arduous and hot. Shorty complained about sore muscles.

"Hey," called Kurt. "I have some powerful liniment that I use for Cindy. Tried it myself. Come to my room, and I'll let you have some."

"Thanks, Kurt. I'm willing to try anything. Be there soon as I wash up."

Shorty finished and went to Kurt's room. He tapped a couple times, opened the door a few inches and called, "Kurt, you in here?"

"Yes," came a voice from the connecting barn. "Go on in. I'm looking for the liniment; I'll be right there."

The room was dark. Shorty, exhausted, took a few steps towards Kurt's bed, tripped, and fell facedown. He had no sooner touched the blanket when Little Tiger, now a full twelve pounds, jumped up on the back of this strange invader and sank its claws. Shorty stood up screaming bloody murder and ran around the room trying to get the cat off his back.

"Get him off!" screamed Shorty. "Get him off! Get this blasted devil off me!"

Kurt ran in and pulled the cat off. When he did, pieces of shirt, skin, and blood came with it.

Shorty ran towards the door and outside.

"Ahhhhhh!"

The mare Cindy came out of the attached corral and chased the running figure of Shorty. The horse took one large bite and bit at the rear end of the cowboy, taking pants, underwear, and a bit of flesh in her teeth.

Shorty ran back through Kurt's room into the open barn and slammed the door shut.

Inside, Kurt tried his best to contain laughter and failed.

"Hell's fire!" shouted Shorty through the door. "I forgot all about your darn critters. Say, this ain't funny. That blasted cat nearly tore my back off, and that devil horse bit me!"

Kurt laughed louder.

"You cayuse! Shut up or I'll come in there and fix you!"

"Alright, go ahead, come on in."

Kurt kept laughing.

"Say, will you shut up?"

Kurt opened the door. He had the cat in his hand.

"Little Tiger, make up with Shorty," said Kurt.

"Little, my eye!"

Kurt held out the cat to sniff Shorty's hand. Tiger hissed and swiped one of his paws, catching Shorty's thumb with a sharp claw.

Shorty roared again.

"Come here, Cindy," called Kurt, "make friends with Shorty."

The mare walked closer, and as she got near him, she began gnashing her teeth and stomping her hooves.

"You keep those darn critters clear of me, understand?" yelled Shorty. "I'm never getting near your crazy animals again. And, if you tell anybody about this, you'll find lead in your backside. Yeah hear?"

That night Shorty came late to dinner. He was wearing a new shirt and pants and walked with a limp. He sat down gently. Food was served out on the patio. After dinner, John asked Shorty if he was feeling well. The cowboy commented that he was a little sore.

Priscilla questioned, "Should I look at what is bothering you?"

Shorty turned red and declined the offer.

"Perhaps some of your discomfiture comes from wearing a cat on your back," said Carlos.

Everyone howled with laughter.

"Or a horse on your butt," added John.

Again they laughed uproariously and kept embellishing the situation with funnier remarks.

"Why, you little rat! You told!"

Shorty jumped up and tried to catch Kurt, but he was in too much pain. The others continued their jocularity.

For a long time, there had been very little to laugh about on Wet Springs Ranch. Eventually, the embellished story reached the ears of the workers and was retold. It took a very long time before Shorty would ever see any humor in the event.

CHAPTER SEVENTEEN

Jedidiah felt twenty years younger.

He talked to anyone who would listen. "That Mrs. West sure fixed me up. My back and shoulder ain't sore no more, and I can go out and do the stuff I was born to do."

Now that Jedidiah had the Sharps with the scope, he could see to shoot again. He hit what he aimed at and at very long distances. To reconnoiter he used a fancy new spyglass and could see far distances just like in his younger days.

The old man started to go out on expeditions, sometimes staying away several days at a time. He was taking seriously his responsibility of helping provide for Wet Springs. Jedidiah began to shoot deer, turkey, and elk. He brought meat home, and Priscilla acted surprised and well pleased. One time he shot a bear. He tanned the hide and gave that to Priscilla. She proudly put it on her bedroom floor.

Jedidiah began to tan the hides of deer in a method he had learned from tribes he had sometimes wintered with. He made heavy moccasins and then switched to making buckskins. He was talented at this, and the set he made were intricately worked. He made several for himself and began to wear them. He now looked like the mountain man he once was.

One day while Jedidiah was out in the hills, he came upon a man spying on the ranch. The old man crept up behind and saw the bushwhacker lift his rifle and take aim at someone bending over near the canyon fence. It was John West. Just like the old days, Jedidiah drew his knife and swiped at the other man's throat. The blade was honed as sharp as a razor, and it nearly took the back shooter's head off.

That night, Jedidiah Taylor came in with a second horse, rifle, and pistol. The Wet Springs crew looked on. They seemed to have a lot more respect for him after that. They knew he killed the man; what they didn't know is that he scalped the back-shooter and put the scalp in the ambusher's mouth. He then placed the dead body in a sitting position with a flat rock on his lap. He had scraped these words on the stone:"No trispassin."

Jedidiah was returning to the man he used to be.

CHAPTER EIGHTEEN

Issy and Kurt, weather permitting, continued the Wednesday picnics with Penelope—when she could slip away. There were times they spent long, lazy afternoons together. Sometimes they had very short visits. The three of them talked about many things and did a lot of hiking, exploring, and riding.

Issy could see from the very beginning that Penelope showed obvious affection for Kurt. She sat next to him by the campfires, she passed food to him first at the picnics, she kept her horse next to his when they rode, and she studied him when she didn't think he noticed. At first, Issy was a little hurt, but he realized how kind Penelope was to keep him with them and not to send him away in order to be alone with Kurt. Besides, he was sixteen, and they were only fourteen. Issy had met a girl through Father Torres; her name was Maria, and she was beautiful.

One Wednesday Issy surprised Kurt by going off and leaving Penelope alone with him. That had never happened before.

"Issy is growing up," said Penelope. "He knew I wanted to be alone with you."

"Why?" asked Kurt naively. "Don't you like Issy?"

"Of course I like him, silly. But I care for you, too. Don't you know that?"

"Yes, we are good friends."

"How can you be so loving and kind to that cat and horse of yours, and not understand women?" Penelope pouted.

"Say what you mean, Penelope; don't beat around the bush."

"Always direct with you, isn't that so? Alright, I'll tell you. My stepfather has been threatening to send me out East, away to school. He tells Mother I am snotty and undisciplined. He says I have too much influence over her."

"I will miss our meetings," said the young man beside her.

"Kurt, is that all you have to say? Hurry, I have to go in a moment. Please keep your cat off me for a minute. Now say something nice."

"I don't know what to say. I like you. I think you are kind and fun to be with."

"Kurt! I'm going to kiss you. This is what you should be doing. Here," Penelope hurriedly put her arms around Kurt, kissed him softly and then fiercely.

"Good-bye, Kurt. I will come back when I can."

The young man watched in amazement as she galloped away. He touched his lips, still feeling her warmth upon them.

CHAPTER NINETEEN

A rumor started. No one knew where it came from and, when mentioned in front of Father Torres, he simply smiled. News was that the famous ranch of Wet Springs would be hosting a fiesta. Riders from town and from distant ranches were soon asking when the party would be held. This bewildered John West and intrigued Priscilla. Finally, together with Father Torres, the dates of July 4th and 5th were set, and a two-day fiesta was planned.

Priscilla made everyone work twice as hard to get the stone pathways completed. She also wanted a wooden platform for dancing to be built behind the house. They met with Father Torres and planned to bring extra help from town. They asked for many musicians so they could alternate playing and so there would always be music. Dancers and singers would entertain while people were eating. Priscilla had the men construct extra benches and tables. They discussed the menu and planned the roasting of several steers and pigs and the preparation of various dishes. It was decided that people would have to bring their own plates and eating utensils. After much debate, Priscilla agreed that only beer and wine would be allowed but no strong liquor. John and Shorty discussed how to handle weapons.

"With that many people together," said John, "there is always the chance that Poindexter will plant men in the crowd who will get tempers riled up and start shooting. You can bet it will be blamed on Wet Springs."

Kurt suggested that guns be left with the saddles or in the wagons. Only the Wet Springs crew would be armed.

The people in town, ranches, and farm families from as far away as fifty miles had heard stories about Wet Springs Ranch. Most wanted to meet the ones who had challenged Poindexter and his gunslingers and survived.

In town, the señoritas wanted to meet the famous Shorty, Kurt, Carlos, and even Issy. They wanted to see the buildings of the ranch and be introduced to Señor and Señora West. Rumors spread about the mountain man, Jedidiah, as well as the other ranch hands from Wet Springs who had successfully fought off the banditos. And most folks laughingly claimed they wanted to see the cat and horse owned by the famous boy gunfighter, Kid Kurt.

La fiesta was going to be a great social event. No one was going to miss it. The exception, of course, would be Poindexter, his followers, and those under his thumb. Some of Poindexter's crew would sneak away anyway, not wanting to miss the excitement. They would attend incognito and make no connection to the powerful but noxious leader.

Several days before the event, wagonloads of ranchers, farmers, and townspeople began to appear. This again bewildered John and Priscilla. Priscilla, Rosa, and Carmen greeted the guests and told them where to park. They placed them far to the east so that there would be room for others as they came. Their horses were put in one of the very large corrals; saddles and tack put on the corral railing or in the large stable. She asked the new guests to mingle and introduce themselves. She inquired if they would need food. It was evident they must acquire more food and cooks. Priscilla sent to town and asked Father Torres to send more workers.

By the morning of the 4th of July, the lower portion of Wet Springs was completely covered. It was a veritable city of wagons, tents, and canvas covers. It was hard to believe there were so many people in the territory. John put the count at near two hundred, with more coming. By nightfall, there may be three or four hundred!

Fortunately, there was sufficient water supplied by the little stream. Sufficient amounts of beef were, of course, available. It would be at greater expense than the Wests expected, but all they had to do was butcher a steer or pig and cook it.

Father Torres arrived with nearly the entire Mexican village. He brought musicians, dancers, helpers, single young men, señoritas, married couples, children, and old people all in their very best and most colorful attire. He also brought the men with the fireworks for the night.

For several days there had been guitar playing, square dancing, and much gaiety around campfires. These impromptu festivities were a complete surprise to the Wests. Priscilla felt they needed to create order out of the chaos and asked Father Torres to help her organize activities. The priest knew his people and their spontaneity. He just smiled.

At noon John and Priscilla, along with Father Torres, gathered at the front of the house. They stood on a platform built for that purpose and asked for quiet. The noise and talking continued until Shorty, seeing his bosses vain attempt, shot his pistol into the air. Quiet blanketed the ranch.

"Helloooo and welcome to Wet Springs Ranch…" announced John West.

Thunderous applause and cheering echoed throughout the crowd.

"On this celebration day of July 4th…" More thunderous applause and shouting resounded. "We welcome you to our home. Please be kind to your neighbor, share, and have fun."

Priscilla stepped forward to talk, and people cheered again, "We want all of you to be safe and happy. Dinner and drinks start now. We will have someone provide entertainment during your meal. First, Father Torres will lead us in a blessing."

Throughout the crowd cowboy hats and sombreros were removed and heads were bowed.

"Ladies and gentlemen," said the priest, "let us pray. Heavenly Father, we thank you for all these gifts you have bestowed upon us today. Grant us peace and happiness on this day of celebration of the independence of our country. Bless the food and the drink we are about to receive. Bless our gracious hosts, Señor and Señora West, and grant them peace and prosperity. May God bless us and grant us a most special fiesta on the Ranch of Wet Springs. In the Name of the Father, and of the Son, and of the Holy Ghost. Amen."

The people screamed and yelled and stomped their feet. A couple of swains shot off pistols; immediately Shorty was there confiscating the revolvers. Kurt, Issy, Carlos, Juan, Jedidiah, Zachery, and many other Mexicans were dispersed throughout the crowd as guards. The 'no weapons' rule was reiterated from the platform by John. Some of this was like talking in a swift breeze. They would have to enforce the rule on a man-to-man basis.

Guests at the Wet Springs fiesta enjoy the entertainment.

A migration began toward the barbecue pits, the massive grilling spits containing turning beef and swine, and the tables with food, beer, and cold drinks. Beside the platform, several Mexican guitar players stood dressed in colorful costumes. A female entertainer appeared in a red ruffled dress with her glistening long black hair swinging coyly over one bare shoulder. She began to sing as she danced, twirling her dress and clicking her shoes as her tall, lean partner matched her staccato beats with his own snapping fingers and graceful movements. Her sultry alto voice permeated the festivities. Her song ended, and there was much applause. By the end of the meal, she had gone through a long repertoire. The crowd loved her.

After lunch, Priscilla asked the guests to rest and prepare for the big dance. Dinner would be served at six o'clock. Those wishing a light repast before dinner could find food set out on the long tables.

During that lazy afternoon, many of the guests wandered around the grounds and looked at the ranch house, the huge barn, and the adobe bunkhouse. They examined the southern corral and its irrigation system. Others walked along the stone paths to the new deck and patio. Many of the older guests sat in the chairs and benches enjoying the cool shelter of the patio roof and gazed across the fields to the canyon in the distance.

The dance had been planned to take place on the patio and on the board floor behind it, but there were too many people. Priscilla did not know what to do. Kurt immediately went to work clearing the animals out of the large barn and having it cleaned by volunteers. By evening the floor was ready and the dance was moved to the huge barn which could accommodate hundreds of dancers, with room for more outside.

"Please, Senor," came repeated calls from the crowd. "Let us see your horse and cat."

Kurt came forward with his pets. He had the mare stand on her hind feet. The young man stood in front of his horse and put out his hand. Cindy raised the right leg and Kurt grasped and shook it. He then led her off the hard stony path and onto the dirt. "Roll over, Cindy!" he said, and the horse complied. He pointed his finger and pretended to shoot toward her. "Bang,!" he said out loud, and she fell over dead," raising all four hooves in the air. The crowd roared.

Little Tiger, who had been waiting by the stone walk, stood erect. Kurt held out his hand and the large cat ran, picking up momentum, and jumped into his arms. The young man set Tiger down and called to Cindy. Kurt started walking away, taking long strides. The cat slinked along behind the horse, which in turn lifted her hooves high as though sneaking up on her owner. They followed him, and he began to run in a circle. The cat jumped on the back of the horse, and the mare continued to follow the young man.

Kurt stopped running, and the horse stopped and stood beside him. He called to the cat, and it jumped on his shoulder. The crowd yelled and whistled. They wanted more.

Kurt asked Cindy to kiss him, and the horse put her muzzle on his cheek. He asked the same of Little Tiger, and the cat nuzzled his owner's cheek. He then patted the horse's back, and the cat jumped there. Then Kurt took the animals back to the stable. The crowd applauded.

Before five the ranch grounds became quiet as the crowd prepared for the big dance. The inhabitants of Wet Springs Ranch were well turned out for the dance. This was an adamant instruction from John to his crew. They were to wear their finest.

Jedidiah Taylor was the first to make his presence known among the crowd. He wore new buckskins and on his feet were Indian moccasins. The fringed shirt he wore had Indian designs and beads worked into the leather. The pants were fringed, and Jedidiah wore a wide leather belt with an enormous buckle. Attached to it was a long Bowie knife in a leather sheath and on the right hip, a fancy nickel-plated pistol in a carved holster. He carried a rifle encased in a leather scabbard delicately fringed, and that too was covered with Indian designs. Crowning his head and long gray hair, was a beaded headband. Jedidiah Taylor looked every bit the mountain man he was fifty years ago.

The crowd took notice of the old man. Here was evidence of the powerful influence the Wests had in bringing out the best in people.

Shorty strutted out, dressed all in black. He wore his special twin holsters and guns. Shorty looked the deadly gunfighter he was. No one was going to make jest of this man and refer to the cat and horse incident to his face.

Kurt wore buckskin pants made by Jedidiah, a sky blue shirt, and a large yellow bandanna. The bandanna was held together with a shiny silver eagle. Kurt had on new boots and a cream-colored hat with a horsehair braid as a hatband. The braid was Penelope's contribution to his attire. And he wore a gun on each hip.

The crowd looked at this youth of fourteen, the kid gunfighter, and gave him respect.

The Wet Springs crew looked their best and yet made it obvious that nonsense would not be tolerated.

The Wests were especially proud of the old man, Jedidiah, and his contributions to the ranch. It was inspiring to see that proud old mountain man strutting before that crowd.

Dr. Bennett arrived on his gift horse, and he seemed as excited as anyone to be part of the festivities. Kurt greeted the doctor and took his horse to the corral and his gear to the back of the house.

Kurt and Issy met the buggy carrying the Schmidts. Mr. Schmidt was rude and ill-tempered and complained to the young men about his wife dragging him to this shindig.

"What's Poindexter going to do when he finds out I came here to Wet Springs?" he continued.

"Look here, Claude, I've had all I'm going to take," responded his wife taking Kurt's hand as he helped the attractive, little lady down from the buggy. "Either you be quiet about that snake, Poindexter, and about business or I'll make you walk home. Pardon me, boys," she said as she saw Kurt grinning, "but thought of that varmint Poindexter brings out the worst in me."

Kurt stood silent next to Mrs. Schmidt.

"Now you listen," she said, addressing her husband once again. "One more word of complaint, and I'll leave you, Claude. You'll never see me again."

"I was just trying to protect our livelihood," said her

husband. "If he finds out about us being here, he'll..."

"That's it. Get away from me, Claude. I mean it. This has been a long time coming. Leave!"

'Priscilla," she said, seeing her friend approach at the sound of the argument. "Would you mind having one of your men saddle him a horse and get him out of here?"

"Kurt," said his mother, "you heard Mrs. Schmidt. Go saddle a horse and escort Mr. Schmidt off the ranch. Issy, you go with him and see that he leaves Wet Springs."

Kurt and Issy went to the corral, caught three horses, and saddled them. The young men mounted and asked Mr. Schmidt to do the same. When he hesitated, Issy put his hand on the butt of his pistol. The stout man climbed up on the horse with difficulty, and the three rode away.

"Thank you, Priscilla," said Mrs. Schmidt as she glared at her husband's departing back. "You don't mind if I spend the rest of my life here, do you? Just kidding, I am sorry for the incident, but today was the last straw. Could I stay a while though?"

"Kate Schmidt, you just stay as long as you want and as long as you need."

At six o'clock, John, Priscilla, and Father Torres got back on the platform. They announced dinner and explained the scheduled festivities. During dinner, entertainment would take place on the platform behind the patio. There would be Mexican dancers and music. After dinner there would be more music and singing. Then the dance inside the large barn would begin.

The crowd cheered its approval. Father Torres blessed

the meal, and then the crowds formed lines at several long tables. Laughter and exclamations of awe were heard as people looked at the amount of food. They took their plates, cups, and utensils and helped themselves to the huge buffet. Music, dancing, and singing continued throughout the entire meal.

Musicians stepped onto a platform in the barn. Before they had finished warming up, the makeshift dance floor was crowded. The music began, and people whooped and cheered. The more boisterous men grabbed willing, and some not so willing partners and swung them onto the dance floor. Lively dancing began in earnest, and it appeared it would stay that way the rest of the night.

The mixture of Mexican and Western styles of music, clothing, and dance was a harmonious riot of color and sound. The Mexican dancers had the most intricate steps, both slow and fast. Every shape, size, and color was moving across the dance floor. Generally, the dancers moved in a huge circle, counterclockwise. The barn was big and there were many partitions. One lost sight of a dancer quickly, and so each view for the onlooker was a new one.

Issy, Kurt, Zachery, Carlos, Shorty, Jedidiah, and John, along with a select group of Mexicans picked by Father Torres, were patrolling the crowd. There was great concern for drunkenness and serious trouble. The huge crowd, many of them strangers, made this concern even more vexing.

By ten o'clock, as the fervor of the night mounted, challenges and squabbles began. Shorty and Jedidiah were best at handling these. They told the offending parties to break it up 'or else'—then to shake hands and go about their business peacefully. Those ruffians who didn't were immediately struck on the head and dragged into the corncrib next to the barn. This had one large, three-inch-thick door. They were thrown onto the corn, and the door was slammed and bolted shut from the outside. They remained there until morning or until it was determined they were ready to be let out.

Already there were drunks in the crowd who were passed out. They had brought their own liquor to the fiesta. Shorty and Jedidiah directed these men to be hauled to the east side of the barn to sleep it off. There they would remain in the dark and out of sight.

At about ten o'clock, a group of twelve horsemen rode directly up to the barn and got down. The crowd backed off and waited to see what would happen. These men were heavily armed, and it was obvious that honest business was not their trade.

A loud whistle alerted the Wet Springs crew. Shorty, Jedidiah, Kurt, Issy, Carlos, Zachery, and John came forward. The crowd let the Wet Springs crew through and there they stood, seven against twelve hard cases. They were no further than fifteen feet apart.

"Good evening, gentlemen," said John. "Welcome to Wet Springs and the fiesta. Before you go into the dance, would you please leave your shooting irons with one of my men? We set up a rule so no one would get hurt. The rule is, no guns."

"You're holdin irons," argued a bearded fellow. He had a scar across one cheek. "You take yours off, and we'll follow."

"Your name?" asked John.

"I'm not in the habit of saying, but they call me Hardy."

"Well, Hardy, we're the ones keeping the peace, so we keep the guns. This is our place, so we make the rules. Shed the pistols, boys, and stay and have a good time. Eat, drink, dance, and have a good time. If you don't give up your revolvers, you're going to have to leave."

"Who's going to…?"

At this point, Kurt pulled his right pistol in a blinding draw. Five shots and five hats flew. He flipped the pistol around and put it in his holster and drew his left-hand weapon. Jedidiah, with a flick of his wrist, shed the rifle sheath, exposed the Sharps rifle and pointed it. Zachery, Issy, Carlos, and Shorty drew their revolvers and stood aiming at the twelve gunmen.

The outlaws backed up.

"Does that answer your question, Hardy?"

"Yup, it shore does. I reckon we just can't shed our weapons cause we'd feel plumb naked. So, we'll just back off for now and be on our way. Maybe we'll meet another time."

The outlaws got back on their horses and rode away.

"Tell Poindexter nice try! We'll be waitin!" yelled out the stentorian voice of Jedidiah.

"Shorty, Poindexter just doesn't give up, does he?" said John.

"He sure don't, boss."

"Kurt, why did you draw and shoot their hats off? That could have started a war."

"Well, Dad, they looked like they were going to draw on us, so I just changed their minds."

Jedidiah chuckled, "I seen a few like Kurt. Relaxed, easygoing, and deadly as a snake. You got a real boy-man, John West. A feller with bite, poison, and fangs."

"Jedidiah, now is not the time," said John. "Alright, how many of you have had a chance to dance? None? Well, I want you to all have a turn. Let Father Torres's people guard for a while. Go on, git."

Issy and Kurt went into the dance together. They stood beside a pillar in the middle of the stable. A very short, pretty Mexican girl came walking over and touched Issy's arm.

"Where have you been?" asked Maria. "I've been waiting all night! Come on, let's dance."

"I'm sorry, Maria; I had to do guard duty for the boss. Do you have a friend to dance with Kurt?"

"If Kurt wishes to dance," she laughed, "I am sure he will have no troubles."

"Go ahead, Issy," said Kurt.

Kurt stood and watched the dancers. He saw Zachery go by with a pretty blonde girl, and then Shorty glided past with an older but quite attractive Mexican lady who danced gracefully. But Kurt's greatest surprise was to see Jedidiah in his mountain finery dancing with an older plump Mexican lady. That old man was full of all kinds of surprises.

To Kurt's delight, he saw Father Torres on the dance floor. Kurt watched his parents go by. How graceful—how young they looked. It was obvious that they were still very much in love. Carlos and Carmen swung past. Obviously, this also was a loving couple. If they were going to give out a prize, Carlos and Carmen would get it. Juan and Rosa danced sedately past, they too, were having fun.

Dr. Bennett passed by, each time with a different partner. Mrs. Schmidt was dancing and obviously having the time of her life. When the music stopped, a long line of eager cowboys was waiting. She accommodated each one, and often others tried to cut in.

Then Kurt noticed a number of females giving him the eye. Around the dance floor girls, daughters of ranchers and farmers were looking towards him. These ladies were very young, some his age. One or two motioned to him with their hands. Kurt was beginning to feel very uncomfortable and was about to leave.

He was tapped from behind on the shoulder. A girl wearing a hat low on her forehead, a white blouse, fringed skirt, and cowboy boots grabbed his hand and pulled him onto the dance floor. Boldly this girl put her arms around Kurt. She guided him into the throng of dancers. The entire time she kept her head tipped down so Kurt could not see her face.

Now the only woman Kurt had ever danced with was his mother. It was she who taught him. This had been part of his school lessons. His mother had told him a man was not civilized until he could dance. Kurt was nervous and uneasy as this young woman held him tightly, not saying a word. Between dances, she kept a tight grip on Kurt's shirt until the music started again. Kurt looked around to see if perhaps Issy or one of the other Wet Springs crew might be responsible for this girl's behavior—maybe as a joke. Slowly his nervousness subsided, and he began to enjoy himself. Still, who was this girl he was dancing with? Why was she wearing a hat? He couldn't see her face.

A slower dance began. The musicians and singers filled the air with sweet melody and harmony. It was a lovely song. Kurt began to walk off the dance floor. The girl grabbed him and glued herself to his body. She danced very slow and closely against Kurt. Who was this? This girl was scaring him. This was going too far.

Kurt reached up and pulled back the hat. Beautiful honey-colored hair fell down around the girl's shoulders. It was Penelope! Quickly Kurt stuck the hat back on her head to disguise her, but already it was too late. There was a great gasp from the crowd and the words, "the Poindexter girl," came to Kurt's ears.

"Penelope, what are you doing here?" he whispered hoarsely.

"You're having a fiesta and didn't invite me?"

"Penelope. Your stepfather will hear about this, and there's no telling what he will do to you."

"That loathsome snake is sending me out East in the morning. To some school in Maryland. I had to see you— and keep the ladies away from you. It looks like I arrived just in time."

Kurt and Penelope made their way through the crowd as they were talking. They came out a side door near his room and walked toward the corral.

"How long will you be gone?"

"Four years. Oh, how I hate my stepfather. Mother will

be lost without me. I am afraid for her. Kurt, I don't trust that man. He is capable of anything."

"I wish I could help. Will you write to me, Penelope?"

"Do you want me to?"

"Of course. I will miss you. Ever since that day, I..."

"Yes?"

"I have had different feelings."

"What I kind of feelings?"

"I worry about you, Penelope. All the time now. I care for you very much...I..."

"It took you long enough," said Penelope.

"I guess it did and I'm sorry for that."

"Promise me, Kurt, that you will write."

"I will."

"Promise me, when I get home from school, you will meet me on Promontory Point."

"I promise."

"Now tell me how you feel about me, Kurt."

"I...I...like you. I..."

Penelope stamped her foot.

"Darn you, Kurt! Do it right!

Kurt's face turned beet red.

"I remember your kiss and your arms around me, and how your hair shone as your hat fell back, your green eyes looking up at mine."

"Yes, Kurt!"

"Your lips felt..."

"Oh, shut up, Kurt, and kiss me."

They stood together in the balmy night, the moonlight shining down almost like day, and this time they kissed open-mouthed. They kissed repeatedly, and both of them learned just how breathless and exciting a kiss and embrace could be.

"I have to go, Kurt. Don't forget me. I'll write. Wait, one more kiss. Good-bye, Kurt. Oh, how I will miss you."

"I will miss you, too, Penelope. Please be careful."

Penelope and Kurt found her horse by the barn. She mounted and spoke softly down to him one more time before she rode away.

"I love you, Kurt West; please don't forget me for another."

Kurt stood there and listened until the drum of the hoof-beats faded away. His mind was in a fog. He barely noticed the throng of people. He walked slowly along the barn. Everywhere he disturbed lovers kissing, hugging, and holding hands in the moonlight. Couples of all ages were airing themselves and finding relief from the heat of dancing and from the crowd.

Kurt found a place to sit and think. *It is obvious that my parents' and Father Torres's fiesta is a great success. And, it isn't even over. Why is it that everything in my life happens before I am really ready for it? Of all the girls to fall in love with, why is it the daughter of my enemy? Why does she have to leave just as I realize what she means to me? Must I and those I care so much about continue to face hardship over and over again? Life seems to be an endless spiral of... Maybe I should go and talk to Father Torres about this? No, I will keep my own thoughts.*

The dance was ending. Pairs of lovers were scattered across the Wet Springs Ranch. Kurt looked up and saw spectacular fireworks, something he had never seen in his entire life. Still, they did not match the fire going on in his heart and mind. Kurt watched as people returned to their campsites.

He went to his room and opened the door. As always, the cat and mare were called from their stable room. He went to them, hugged them, and in their way, they hugged him back. Cindy was let out to her special corral. Kurt removed and hung up his clothes. He lay down on the bed and pulled a sheet and blanket up over himself. Little Tiger jumped up on Kurt's chest, circled twice and lay down. Kurt petted the cat, and the cat put his head under Kurt's neck and began to purr. After a long time, the young man fell asleep.

The next morning people slept late. Breakfast was served between eight and ten o'clock. At ten a rifle shooting contest started; anyone who wanted to enter was welcome with the exception of the Wet Springs crew—their responsibility was to officiate. By noon most contestants were screened and assigned to various competitions.

Many targets had been lined up in a row to speed the contest along. By afternoon, with just eight contestants left, they were using one target at a distance of a hundred yards. The object was to hit the bulls-eye three shots in a row. Contestants could use any type of rifle they wanted. There were four prizes to be awarded from one-hundred down to twenty-five dollars.

Very quickly the contestants were whittled down to four. Jedidiah moved the target to two hundred yards, and the shooters complained. He moved it forward to one hundred fifty and very quickly first, second, third, and fourth winners were determined. The prize money was handed out, and the crowd cheered.

Someone yelled for the mountain man to shoot. Others picked it up until everyone was shouting. John, having no idea what the old man could do, was undecided. Jedidiah raised his hand for silence.

"My eyes ain't what they use to be, so I'll use a scope. I'll hit the bulls-eye with three shots at two hundred yards, and at five hundred."

Kurt and Issy each came forward to help. Issy rode a target out to two hundred yards and Kurt to five hundred. Both rode off some distance to wait and retrieve the targets.

Jedidiah took out the Sharps with the scope and aimed at the two hundred yard bulls-eye. He squeezed the trigger, and the single-shot .50 caliber rifle kicked at the old man's shoulder. Jedidiah loaded, aimed, and shot two more times. Issy rode up, yanked off the piece of thick paper and raced for the contest line. He handed the paper to John. With some trepidation, John examined it. Three holes pierced the black center. John held it up and turned in a circle for the crowd to see. They cheered.

Jedidiah took aim at the second target—out five hundred yards—over fifteen hundred feet. Boom! The big gun went off. Carefully, taking his time, Jedidiah loaded, aimed and fired twice more. With each shot, he gently squeezed the trigger, and the rifle seemed to go off on its own.

Kurt raced the horse back with the target in his hand. He handed it to his father. John looked and noted one hole in the exact center. Another bullet hole was on the center line, and so was the third shot. John shook his head in amazement as he held the target up. The crowd again roared. The winner of the previous contest declined to try to duplicate Jedidiah Taylor's marksmanship.

On the way to lunch, those who could spoke to Jedidiah and congratulated him. Some tried to thump him on the back. Jedidiah touched the big Bowie knife, and that sort of behavior stopped.

Father Torres said grace and the crowd ate. By two o'clock, John got up on the platform and tried to shout thanks to everyone for coming. People cheered and applauded, and then reluctantly began to pick up and leave. People agreed that it was a great dance, a muy bueno fiesta, a wonderful gathering of friendship and boisterous amusement.

CHAPTER TWENTY

The next two years passed slowly for Kurt. He missed the Wednesdays with Penelope more than anything else in his life. He often rode Cindy to Promontory Point and Tiger, always accompanying, would jump down and follow him up to sit on the rock where Penelope, Issy, and he had so often sat and talked. Kurt would gaze absently over the ranch and then turn his head due east to where miles and miles away lay Maryland and the girl he loved.

Jedidiah had fashioned a cat-saddle for Little Tiger. It was made out of several layers of soft deerskin with a hole in it to fit over the saddle horn. Tiger would jump up in front of Kurt and bury his claws in the leather in order to hang on when the horse galloped. He and his animal friends went everywhere together, inseparable as always. He felt as if they were almost a part of him. Their company eased his loneliness.

Life at Wet Springs went on as usual. New respect for Jedidiah gave credence to his warnings that men were hanging around the place and looking for a chance to do some damage. Occasionally Jedidiah rode in with another horse and gear. This gave evidence that the bushwhacker who attempted to shoot at someone on the ranch met with a fatal end. The old man didn't tell them he was scalping these men and leaving warning messages on rocks.

Perhaps Wet Springs owners didn't realize it, but the once drunken old man had again become a toothsome old lion. He was, in fact, worth his weight in gold as he made his daily excursions and rides around the ranch. His overnight trips frequently caught Poindexter's invaders by surprise and Jedidiah was often given opportunities to test his marksmanship. The Sharps .50 left many a wounded or dead gunfighter to be carried back to Poindexter's ranch by his companions.

One time the old man had been north in the hills; he was coming back from an elk hunt and carrying the best meat wrapped in its hide on a packhorse. Jedidiah had worked out a trail where he could get in the mountains without traveling on foot. Several miles ahead, Jedidiah saw a group of about fifteen men coming from the east, using the cover of rocks, and heading for the massive iron gate at the canyon's mouth. The time was early morning, before sunup. Jedidiah worked his way forward. A half mile from the men, he tied off the two horses and made his way further on foot.

The old man took a trail up a wall of rock that overlooked the canyon and the fence. The mountain man lay down on the edge and looked below to where the intruders were attempting to plant dynamite at the gate. No time to lose, Jedidiah took a leather bag from his shoulder, set it down, reached in, grabbed fifteen or twenty of the large-caliber bullets, and placed them next to him. He aimed at a man lighting a match and shot him through the chest. As fast as Jedidiah could, he loaded the rifle and fired at the men around the gate. The rustlers sought cover, but the mountain man was high up, several hundred yards away, and at an angle where the fence provided little shelter. Jedidiah kept on shooting, and men kept on dying from large gaping wounds.

The remaining rustlers got on their horses and rode east as fast as they could go. Jedidiah still didn't stop firing. He kept right on loading and shooting men off their horses as they tried to get away. His last few shots were at some thousand yards, over three thousand feet away. Horses and men were still being hit.

Jedidiah heard pounding of horse's hooves coming from way off by the ranch. That would be the crew, having heard the racket.

"Let them see this here; they'll believe me now."

Jedidiah turned around and made his way down the trail and went back to get his horses. He mounted up and headed toward the canyon mouth. The old man could see John and the rest of the crew walking around examining the dead men. Jedidiah rode up and dismounted.

"These pilgrims tried to blow your fence. I persuaded them not to. The dynamite is over there by the gate, next to that dead feller with the burnt fingers."

John just looked at the mountain man in amazement. "You did this?" he asked.

"Me and old Betsy Sharps, the longest, best shooting gun there is."

"It's a hard thing you did," said John.

"Hard, but necessary, boss," replied Shorty.

"Tell us what happened," said Carlos.

"I was coming back, packing this here elk. I stayed overnight and got up early. It was too cold to sleep in. When I was a couple miles from here, I saw a group of riders makin' their way to the canyon. I got closer and spied what they was doing. One feller had that there dynamite, so I shot 'em. Kinda went natural after that. I carries a lot of ammunition, so I kept shootin. Figure maybe nine dead and three or four wounded. Way east, I hit a horse, probably killed it. Feel bad about that. That's about the size of it."

"That's plenty, Jedidiah," said John. "I'm sure glad you're on our side. Anything else?"

"Well, you being the boss and all, you probably already figured out if they thought of dynamite they're gettin plumb mean. If they do it again, it's sure going to make some mess."

"Darn right," said Shorty. "Boss, we'll have to patrol all the time now."

"We don't have enough riders for that, Dad," said Kurt.

"We'll just have to make do with what we got. Jedidiah, are you up to guarding full time? We'll pay you workman's wages, whatever extra you think is fair. You sure saved the cattle this time."

"And the horses, too, Dad."

"I reckon if Mrs. West makes up some more of that liniment, and gives me a hot toddy now and then, that's enough to keep me going," drawled Jedidiah.

For the next year, the ranch was guarded round the

clock by the Wet Springs hands. Jedidiah taught Zachery how to shoot the Sharps. The rest carried .44 rifles. There were occasional skirmishes and running fights but nothing like the one that day at the canyon with Jedidiah.

It seemed that only the old man could sneak up on a Poindexter man unaware. The mountain man lived up to his name. Several other outfits, horses, and guns were brought in by him, evidence of one less enemy for Wet Springs.

CHAPTER TWENTY-ONE

Kurt was now seventeen and Issy nineteen. They would sometimes saddle up like they were going to camp out on the range, but as evening approached, would sneak into town to the Mexican side. Issy would meet his girlfriend, Maria, and Kurt would be introduced to one of her many friends. Kurt was polite but noncommittal. The girls gradually lost interest. There soon came a time when it began to be a habit for Kurt to find Father Torres and talk to him.

The priest knew this boy was risking his life to ride into town like this and asked why he took such a chance if he was not interested in one of the girls. Kurt explained he did it for his friend. The priest asked him if it was normal to risk one's life so his friend could see a girl. Kurt responded, "That's what friends do for one another."

At first Father Torres and Kurt talked of surface things: the ranch and its activities. Then on later visits, they talked about personalities, and there was much joking about Shorty, Jedidiah, and even Kurt himself. They talked of the never wavering convictions of his parents. Of how strong and unbending his mother was and how understanding his father.

Finally, they began to discuss Poindexter and his control over so many people; this became a long talk about right and wrong, good and evil. They conjectured on who would win in the end. Although Father Torres put it more academically, they agreed that one must keep trying to do the right thing, to stay with one's convictions until one's life ended. To do anything less meant that life was compromised, cheapened, and perhaps made meaningless.

On another visit, Father Torres astutely asked if Kurt had a special friend, one who involved the affairs of the heart. Before Kurt realized it, he was telling Father Torres about Penelope—how he had first seen her in the church, how he had met her nearly every week at Promontory Point, and how she had sworn she loved him at the fiesta. She had made him promise to meet her at their secret rendezvous when she got back. It had been three years now, and she was the only girl he thought about. One more year and they would both be eighteen and together again.

"Four years is a very long time, Kurt," said Father Torres. "Even though people make promises, their feelings change, circumstances change. Maybe she will have different thoughts about you."

"I don't think so, Father. Here, see this letter I keep. Penelope writes to me in care of Mrs. Schmidt—I mean Mrs. Bennett—now that she married Doc. No one knows about the letters, and Doc's wife is sworn to secrecy. I will not show you the letter, but she says she still loves me. She writes of how arrogant and foolish people can be back East, and she can't wait to return. Tell me, Father Torres. What am I to do? I am in love with the daughter of my family's worst enemy."

"I don't know, my son, but I believe you must have faith. Faith as strong as your love for this young lady so many thousands of miles away."

CHAPTER TWENTY-TWO

It was a very hot day in July, almost a year later. There had been little activity on Poindexter's side and guarding the perimeters of Wet Springs had relaxed. One project that John West wanted completed was to replace a long section of the fence up against the canyon.

Off and on, the workers, along with Kurt, Issy, Juan, Carlos, Shorty, and John, helped break and carry stone. Jedidiah was still guarding. One particular afternoon the old man found a cool spot high up in the rocks and took a little siesta. Some of the crew were at the ranch eating lunch. John, along with Shorty, Kurt, and Issy were just breaking from a good morning's work and making ready to ride in for lunch.

A single gunshot exploded, and the sound reverberated throughout the canyon and made its way to the ranch house. Priscilla, who was preparing lunch, dropped a plate on the table and ran for her medical bag. Then racing to the corral, she grabbed a worker's saddled horse and rode for the canyon. Only one gunshot, but...

When Priscilla arrived, John was lying with his head on Kurt's lap—blood pooling on the ground.

"No, John," she screamed, jumping from the saddle. "No!"

"Calm down, Mother," pleaded Kurt, fighting tears.

"The dirty cowards," said Priscilla tearfully. "The dirty..."

Kurt was holding his father, trying to stop the bleeding with a kerchief. Gently Priscilla turned her husband's head and looked at the gaping wound at the back of his neck. Both Kurt and his mother could see part of the spine and broken bits of bone. Priscilla fought back nausea. It was different when it was someone you love.

Get a grip and don't let go, she told herself. *His only chance is you.*

Quickly she opened her bag, took out bandages, and applied a compress on the wound. Then wrapped it as tightly as she dared. She stood up and spoke very authoritatively—fighting to keep her voice from shaking.

"He has a spinal injury. He cannot be moved. Shorty, ride for the ranch, come back with a long board as wide as a man. We have to tie his head down and then carry him to the house. Kurt, you take your horse and three of the thoroughbreds and ride for Dr. Bennett. If you keep switching mounts, you should get there in a few hours. Put the doctor on a horse and get him back here as soon as you can. Have him switch mounts too. Now Kurt listen; make sure the doctor knows it's a spinal injury in the neck. Describe it to him. Make certain he brings what he needs, or we're wasting our time. I'm counting on you. Be careful!" she said, giving him a quick, tight hug.

Kurt jumped on Cindy and was gone. Tiger raced after

Kurt and the horse. At the stable Kurt put Tiger in his room and Cindy in her corral. Kurt saddled three thoroughbreds. Carmen brought him a canteen and a little bag of food. She, too, gave Kurt a hug and whispered, "Via con Dias."

Shorty, with help from Carlos, found a suitable board and rode back to the canyon with it. The men took turns carrying John to the house with Priscilla monitoring every step of the way. It took a long time to carry him by foot to the ranch house. They took him into the kitchen and laid him on the long table. He blinked and opened his eyes.

"Priscilla."

"Yes, John. Now be still. Don't move. You were shot. Do you know this?"

"Hard to speak."

"Oh, John, hang on. I sent Kurt for the doctor. I have the bleeding stopped. Don't you dare give up on us; we need you. Doctor Bennett will fix you up when he gets here."

"I can't feel anything, Priscilla. I would rather be dead than live like this. Don't cry. We had twenty-three good years. Did you know it was that long?"

"Oh, John. God help me, but I can't make it better," Priscilla sobbed. "John, I don't know what to do."

"Not even you can fix everything. I'm going now, my love. Say good-bye to Kurt. I love you both very much, and I was always so very proud..."

Air escaped his lungs in a long gentle sigh.

Priscilla lost control—she, who had always been so strong. Her sobbing scared the others with its intensity. She cried and beat her fists on the table, injuring her hands.

"John! Wake up, honey. John, wake up! I never really told you how much…"

She fainted. Shorty jumped and caught her before she hit her head on the floor. He carried her to the couch in the living room. The Wet Springs women cried, and the men looked on in distress. John West lay dead on the kitchen table.

CHAPTER TWENTY-THREE

The shot startled Jedidiah Taylor and awoke him from his
dreams. There was nothing wrong with his hearing. The
location, the single shot, made it that much more ominous.
It was unlikely that someone accidentally discharged
a rifle, not near the canyon mouth where the crew was
working. Could a back-shooter have gotten on that high
rock above the fence and shot down on someone? If that
was the case, it was a Poindexter man, and he would be
heading east back to his ranch.

Jedidiah ran, walked, and then slid off the high rocks
down to his horse. He headed south then turned on a trail
heading east. He hoped to cut off the gunman, if he wasn't
too late. The old man's gut sinking feeling was that his
instincts were all too right and that something tragic had
occurred.

Jedidiah's horse stumbled and slipped backwards on a
granite slope. The older man jumped down, grabbed the
reins, and pulled the mount up and over rock. From this
rise the mountain man saw a horse and rider, traveling at a
gallop. It came out from a jumble of stones on Wet Springs
property. The old man only had seconds to determine what

to do. He grabbed the Sharps and aimed over six hundred yards at the fleeing gunman. He pulled the trigger and the horse fell. The rider flew through the air and landed in a heap. It looked like the horse was hit in the head and died instantly. Jedidiah would go check on the rider.

When the mountain man got up close, it wasn't a pretty sight. The man was lying on his side, and his neck was twisted in a funny angle.

"You got to help me, mister," said the gunman. "I can't move my waist or my legs."

"Sure I'll help you, young one, just as soon as you tell me what you did over on Wet Springs."

"I didn't do nothin. Hey, where you going?"

"I ain't going to help no liar. Now you tell me what you did."

"Please mister."

"I won't help no back-shooter, but I'll sit here and watch the buzzards feed on you while you're still alive."

"I'm scared. I don't want to die like this."

"Don't tell me your life story, sonny, just what happened."

"Poindexter sent me. He told me to shoot John West. He promised a pile of money if I did."

"Did you do it?"

"Yes."

"Say your prayers! Your neck's busted and you're dying. What you want? Kill you or leave you alive for the buzzards?"

"You said you would help me."

"John West was my boss."

"Then kill me. Shoot me in the head, so I don't feel nothin."

Jedidiah pulled his big Bowie and bent down and slit the man's throat. There was gurgling and flowing blood.

"A bullet is too much to waste on you, boy."

The tough old man grabbed the bushwhacker's holster and pistol and took the rifle off the dead horse. He mounted and headed back to the ranch.

At the house, Jedidiah Taylor wearily got off his mount, dropped the reins, and walked through the patio to the back door. He knocked, then opened the screen and walked in. There lay John West, dead on the table. Carmen and Rosa were crying. Priscilla lay on the couch. Jedidiah felt moisture in his eyes, something he hadn't known since a youngster. He hesitantly started toward Priscilla to tell her how bad he felt and how he had failed her. But when he reached the couch, he could see she wasn't in her right mind.

Shorty came over, took Jedidiah's arm, and led him outside.

"This is the feller's rifle and pistol," the old man said, wiping his face. "Danged, got something in my eye. This here rifle is what he shot Mr. West with."

"Did you get the cur?"

"It was a long shot at a running horse. The animal fell and the shooter was still alive, his neck broken. He confessed, then I slit his throat."

"Guess he paid. We're waiting for the doctor. Priscilla sent for him, but it looks like she's the one who's going to need care. Never saw a woman carry on so. Pretty near killing her losing John like this. It's a terrible thing. After the funeral we ought to do something—make Poindexter pay."

Shorty walked away. Jedidiah had already made up his mind what he was going to do. It was his fault John was dead and Mrs. West was lying in there out of her mind. He would do what a Plains Warrior used to do: make a last stand and fight the Poindexter crew on their own ground.

Jedidiah went and asked Carmen to fix enough food for him to last four days. He told her he was going in the hills to guard the ranch. Carmen was relieved to have a task to perform. The mountain man went back to the adobe bunkhouse and removed the table covering the entrance to the tunnel. The old man took a lantern to the storage area and rummaged for .50 caliber ammunition. He filled a sack with three hundred rounds. That, combined with his present supply, added up to four hundred. Jedidiah also took a .44 Winchester, pistol, and extra ammunition.

Back outside, the mountain man saddled a fresh horse, tied the heavy saddlebags on its back, fastened down a bedroll and the food that Carmen had prepared. Then he hung three large canteens on the saddle horn. The .44 rifle he put in a saddle scabbard and the Sharps he carried in his hand. Jedidiah mounted and headed straight east.

Riding very slowly because of the weight, and desiring to reach Poindexter's ranch near dark, he took his time. The old man sat on the saddle and thought of all the events that had occurred to him since he had met the Wests. *They cleaned me up and gave me new clothes and self-respect. They gave me a horse, saddle, a Sharps, and a pistol—*

all before they knew what I could do with them. At the big party, they let me parade in my finery, and they were proud of me. I got to show that I was a man again in front of those people. They let me shoot. They trusted me. With the care I got and the operation on my back, I perked right up. Strong enough to guard and do what was needed. And now, when they most counted on me, I fell asleep in the rocks and a killer invaded and shot John West. I'll take care of that mistake now...so help me and my maker.

Jedidiah took low ground and walked his horse near Poindexter's ranch. He scouted the land and located a clump of rocks. It was about four hundred yards from the bunkhouse. Still taking the low ground, he walked his horse near the base of the hill and dismounted. He took the weapons, the saddlebags, food, and climbed the hill and got in among the rocks. It was perfect. Just like a fort. He went back down and got his bedroll and canteens. He debated what to do with the horse and, in respect to the beast, he whumped it hard on the rump, and it headed back for Wet Springs.

There was still plenty of afternoon left, so methodically Jedidiah laid out the ammunition, rifles, canteens, food, and bedroll. He checked out each rock in a circle and scanned the land and horizon. It was a lot of land to cover by one man, but if he was alert, it could be done. The Sharps was the secret to the whole thing. Keep 'em back, don't let them get close.

Jedidiah took out the spyglass and laid it down on the top of a flat rock. He chewed on some jerky and then scoped several buildings. Men were coming into the corral and unsaddling horses and knocking off for the day. Jedidiah wanted to catch them after supper when they were lounging in the bunkhouse.

The mountain man waited. He broke open boxes of ammunition and piled shells loosely in the leather saddlebags. The old man tried to quit thinking the self-loathing thoughts. It was a mantra in his head. He could not forget the picture of Priscilla West, the only woman who really cared about him. She helped a sick old man gain his self-respect. He loved her for it. And now because of his failure to keep alert, his boss was dead and Mrs. Priscilla out of her mind. Clearly, John West's death was his fault. Today, he would try his best to do what he could to protect those still living on Wet Springs Ranch.

Just before dusk, Jedidiah Taylor saw groups of men near one bunkhouse. He saw another building near it that also seemed to be quarters for ranch hands. He could also see the cook shack and dining area. He was ready. Once started, he knew how this would end. To achieve his goal, he must stay alive as many days as possible. An old man, he had lived a long life. Nothing could correct his great failure, but this was something he knew he could do.

"About time someone took the battle to them," he whispered out loud.

The big boom of the Sharps in the twilight startled every living creature within five miles. Jedidiah just kept on firing. He riddled the first bunkhouse with several rounds and then moved to the cook shack, dining area, and then the other end of the sleeping quarters. Jedidiah fired fifty rounds each into the buildings and then stopped. No question they knew where he was, the muzzle flash was tremendous. No doubt they thought he was gone by now. Wait until morning.

"Dang-it," he muttered, "my shoulder sure is sore. Not like the old days when I could fire all day long at those buffalo."

CHAPTER TWENTY-FOUR

By eight-thirty that evening, Dr. Bennett and Kurt arrived at the ranch. Mrs. Bennett was on her way in a buggy with Father Torres and two Mexican guards.

Kurt followed Dr. Bennett into the house. It was immediately evident to the doctor and Kurt that his father was dead. The young man's stomach turned ice cold. He watched the doctor approach his mother. She lay on the couch and was mumbling to herself. Dr. Bennett tried to talk to her to no avail. Kurt could see that his mother was out of her head.

"How long has she been like this?" asked Dr. Bennett.

"Since John died," answered Shorty. "I've never seen anyone fall apart this bad."

"Shock. This can be very serious. I'll give her something to make her sleep. The next two days are critical; my wife and I will stay."

Kurt felt numb and confused, not sure what there was for him to do. He walked out of the house. This was it. Enough was enough. He went back to his rooms, lit a lantern and rummaged for his shoulder holster and pistols. He took several boxes of ammunition and piled them on the bed. He packed some clothes into a bag.

"Think," he said aloud. "Use the brains God gave you."

Kurt took the tunnel entrance from the stable to a place beneath the house. He picked up empty saddlebags, removed a stone from the wall, a hiding place known only by his father and mother, and pulled out a metal box. Kurt opened it and took out two thousand dollars. He returned the remaining bundle of money and replaced the stone. Putting the cash in the saddlebags, he went back to his room.

Kurt took the clothes and ammunition he had left on his bed and stuffed them in the saddlebags. He strapped on a shoulder holster and now wore three pistols. Then he made sure Cindy and Tiger were locked in the stable in the barn. He carried the bags to the corral, lassoed and saddled a thoroughbred, tying the saddlebags to the cantle. Kurt rode to the log barracks and stopped. He called to one of the workmen.

"Diego, yesterday you came back from town and you told me you saw Poindexter."

"Si, Señor Kurt, Poindexter spends much time at his new saloon. Father Torres says he has rooms there."

"You're sure of this?"

"Si, Señor."

"Will you feed my animals?"

"Si, are you going to town alone?"

"Yes," replied the young man.

Kurt stopped at a building used for storing dynamite. Opening the door, he stepped in. He took two sticks, a cap, and fuse, and placed them in one of his saddlebags.

Shorty, shocked and depressed, didn't pay attention when Kurt rode in with the doctor. It was Issy who told him that something was up with Kurt and that he had just ridden out on one of the thoroughbreds. Shorty jerked out of his lethargy.

"Issy, get your stuff. Carlos! Guns and horses!" he roared.

Issy had learned from the worker that Kurt had asked for his animals to be fed and that he had gone to town. Shorty, Carlos, and Issy quickly saddled and rode as fast as they could in pursuit.

Cindy and Little Tiger must have sensed something was bothering their master. Perhaps it was that the workman startled the mare and cat when he went to feed them. What the man got instead of hungry animals was an angry mare kicking the lower half of the Dutch door. It broke open. Cindy rushed past, knocking the man down. A flash of fur and the tiger-striped cat ran full speed after the mare and jumped on her back, sinking his claws into the mare's hide. Together they raced in the direction their master had ridden.

Kurt arrived with a lathered horse. It was near midnight. He dismounted, took the dynamite out of the saddlebags, and walked towards the saloon. In his anger, Kurt's intent was to blow it up. After all, that's what they tried to do to his father's ranch. Kurt changed his mind, stuffed the dynamite in his shirt, and went in the open doors. He needed to gather his thoughts. If anyone wanted to confront him, let them try.

Kurt paused and waited for his eyes to adjust to the dim

light. There at the bar was Sheriff Engler and a deputy. Sitting at a table at the far wall were Poindexter, the banker, a merchant, and an unknown gambler. Standing against the wall looking on were three of Poindexter's guards. When they recognized Kurt West, they pulled their revolvers. Kurt, drawing and fanning his right pistol, shot the three of them in the chest. Such fast and precise shooting surprised everyone in the saloon.

Sheriff Engler began a clumsy draw, and the deputy just stared.

"Throw down your guns, boys. All of you! NOW!" ordered Kurt, pointing his pistol.

The bartender came up from behind the counter, leveling the barrel of a shotgun. Kurt shot him in the chest, the shotgun went off, dropping a burst of wood and plaster from a hole in the ceiling. The bartender disappeared back behind the bar.

Sheriff Engler and the deputy threw down their guns.

"You cowards!" yelled Poindexter.

"You'll have a chance to respond to that, you snake," growled Kurt. "Right now, I'm interested in what kind of guns the rest of you have. No fooling! Shuck `em!"

The banker threw a derringer on the floor, the businessman swore he had no gun, and the gambler tossed down a shoulder pistol and, on second thought he pulled out a sleeve gun and threw it on the table before him.

"Good. Now, Poindexter. You were talking about cowards. I have three pistols here. Which one do you want?"

"I'm not a gun slick. You'd have the advantage."

"Yeah, but you hire gun slicks. You hang around with them. You tell them what to do. You sent one, and he killed my father. So, as they say, live by the gun, die by the gun. Now pick one, or I'll shoot you."

"No, I won't do it...besides, I think you better look around."

"Reach, Kid," said a voice from behind.

"No, you fools!" yelled Poindexter. "Shoot him! Shoot him in the back! Cut him down!"

Kurt heard the click of a cocking gun and turned his head. There were two men standing there with drawn pistols ready to kill. What happened next amazed even Kurt. A furry object jumped up on the shoulder of one gunman and began clawing at the man's face. The fellow started screaming and ran out the bat-wing doors to the street.

The other gun-hand was attacked from behind by the mare who came clattering into the barroom and bit down on his shoulder. Cindy almost picked him up in her teeth, and then shaking her head, threw him on the floor. The horse reared up and crushed the man's head.

Kurt turned back in time to see the sheriff reach for a hide-out pistol. The young man shot him in the arm.

There came the pounding of horses' hooves. Shorty, Carlos, and Issy rode up in time to see a man with a cat on his face, struggling in the street. Poindexter's man dislodged the cat and threw it. Tiger struck against a post and landed in the dust. The gunman's face was scratched and bloody. He had a second pistol, and he drew it. Shorty shot him in the head from his standing horse.

The three men dismounted and raced into the bar. They saw the mare snuggling Kurt and the young man trying to push her away. It was impossible to miss the stomped body on the floor. They also saw the three dead men in the corner, as well as the wounded sheriff. The deputy, Poindexter, the banker, the merchant, and the gambler stood with hands raised.

"Looks like you've been busy, Kurt," said Shorty. "Couldn't wait for your friends?"

"This was something I had to do. Couldn't ask you to risk it. By the way, I'm glad to see you."

"Right," said Issy. "Sometimes, Kurt, you go too far."

"What you do, we do, amigo," said Carlos.

"Hold on, boys, I have a little unfinished business," continued Kurt as he aimed his pistol at Poindexter. "Now, pick a weapon."

"I won't do it."

Kurt walked over and pistol-whipped the man, one sharp smack across the face.

"I'll kill you right here, you coward," said Kurt.

Poindexter remained motionless, blood trickling from a cut in his cheek. Kurt approached the sheriff.

"Engler, you crooked paid-for rodent. Give me that badge. You don't deserve to wear it!"

Kurt reached with his left hand and ripped it off the sheriff's shirt and put it in his pocket.

"After tonight, if I ever see you again, I'll kill you. You understand?"

"Yes," replied Engler holding his bloody arm.

Kurt returned to where Poindexter stood.

The town ruler didn't move. Kurt grabbed hold of his shoulders and, to his surprise, the cadaverous man had strong, sinewy muscles. The young man pulled the coward's arms behind his back, grabbed his handkerchief, and tied his wrists. Then he took the dynamite out of his shirt, cap and fuse attached. This he stuck down behind the belt of Poindexter's pants.

"Little extreme, Kurt, don't you think?" asked Shorty.

"That's the whole point, Shorty, no thinking, just doing. I almost forgot. Poindexter, you have one week to clear out, or I will be coming for you. If I find you in this town or on your ranch one week from now, you're a dead man. That goes for your crew and any friend of yours left in this town. Mr. Gambler, you spread the word in case Poindexter forgets. Now, somebody give me a match."

No response.

"I will shoot everyone in this bar in the foot until someone gives me a blasted match."

The gambler took one from his pocket and handed it to Kurt. The young man lit the lucifer and started the foot-long fuse sputtering.

"The object of this game, Poindexter, is to show you how dangerous dynamite can be. I wonder if you have a friend in this room who cares enough to save your life. Come on, Cindy, let's go."

Kurt walked out followed by his horse. Shorty, Carlos, and Issy followed, then hurriedly came the businessman, the banker, the sheriff, and the deputy. They listened. No explosion. The young gunman grimaced, the only person with sand among that group was the gambler.

Kurt could feel his knees trembling. He hoped no one noticed him shake. Then he saw his cat lying in the road. He ran to Tiger and touched him gently. The left front leg seemed to be hurt. Kurt picked up his cat and with his horse, started towards the Mexican quarters.

Carlos and Issy grabbed Kurt's other mount.

"See that he's looked after, I rode him hard," he said.

From there, the four went to Issy's girlfriend's house. A young Mexican led the mounts away. The girl's father gently took the injured cat from Kurt's arms.

Then Maria's father carefully bandaged the leg and said, "Don't worry, Señor Kurt, I will make el gato much better."

The four were given a place to sleep. In the morning they were served breakfast, and then they retrieved their horses and rode to the train station. The injured cat was left in the care of Maria's father.

Kurt bought tickets to Denver for the four of them. He told the agent he wanted a boxcar for their horses. The agent laughed. Shorty told him who Kurt was and the man promptly pointed to a boxcar sitting on a spur. Kurt paid the extra fee, and the horses were loaded. Within a half-hour, the train arrived, and the boxcar was attached. The West crew boarded a passenger car.

"Alright, I'll bite," said Shorty. "What are we gonna do in Denver?"

"We're going to do what we should have done a long time ago, hire gunfighters."

"So, we're going to be just like Poindexter?"

"No, we're going to hire good men who just happen to

be good with guns. There's a difference."

"How do we find such men, Señor Kurt?" asked Carlos.

"Simple, you'll interview and hire them."

"Seems like a tall task," said Issy.

A man dressed in a business suit said sarcastically to his companion, "Look at that cowboy's guns."

"Shut up, you fool," hissed the other. "That's Kid Kurt, you want to get us killed?"

Despite themselves, Kurt's companions smiled.

Hours later the train pulled into the Denver Station. The men went to the boxcar, unloaded their horses, and headed to one of the stables. This was virtually a boomtown, and every imaginable kind of building was going up. There were false fronted stores of cut lumber, some permanent brick buildings, fancy saloons, hotels, new framed construction, and various businesses behind framed tarps.

The people were even more diverse. There were men and women still in Eastern clothing. There were dancehall girls in bright dresses; there were sturdy farm women walking down the street with baskets of produce on their hips, and there were even some women hanging over railings. Cowboys, businessmen, carpetbaggers, salesmen, Indians, gunslingers, cattlemen, and foreigners of every description moved along boardwalks. There were Chinese, Swedes, Irish, Russians, Finnish, Norwegian, and others— many dressed in clothes from their homelands speaking in their own languages. It was a cacophony of sound and color. The railroad was filling up the west.

The four stabled their horses. Kurt took the men to a fancy hotel, and they checked in and got two rooms. Kurt paid in advance upon request and then asked to rent a couple of meeting rooms—one large and one small. He explained to the hotel manager that they would be interviewing men for employment. They needed a large room for them to wait in and a smaller one for the interview. The hotel employee said something about it being expensive. The manager's eyes widened as Kurt drew gold coins from a pocket.

"This will be fine," said the hotel clerk, "you can start using the rooms tomorrow morning."

The four walked into the dining room and stopped in amazement. The sparkling chandeliers and huge paintings on the walls were displays of elegance they had never seen before. A waiter took them to a table where they sat down and were handed menus. Carlos and Shorty took one look and set the menus down.

"Issy, perhaps you would like to order something for your father."

"Say, Kurt, order old Shorty whatever you're havin'."

Kurt and Issy smiled at each other. When the waiter came, Kurt ordered coffee, steak, champignons, and a variety of side orders."

"He calls that simple," mumbled Shorty.

CHAPTER TWENTY-FIVE

Poindexter sat in the back office of his newly acquired saloon and radiated rage. That kid dared to touch his person and upset his plans. Poindexter's brain fairly boiled.

"How dare that boy touch me!" he swore. "And that woman, the Kid's mother, did it too, years ago in that church. I should have taken care of her then. It took long enough, but she paid for it, her man's dead. Now, to get rid of the nit!"

A man barged into his office and Poindexter grabbed a paperweight and threw it at his ranch foreman. Billings turned sideways, and it hit him in the thigh.

"Boss! That hurt!"

"Don't ever come barging through that door again! Knock! Now, what do you want?"

"You're not going to like it."

"There are lots of things I don't like after last night. Spill it."

"Several men are out in the rocks firing down on the ranch."

"What? They're shooting up my house? My mansion?"

"No, Boss, for some reason they're leaving the big

house alone, but they're shooting everything else. They shot up the barracks, the cookhouse, the dining area, and the foreman's quarters. Boss, it's shot to pieces. Big caliber bullets. We've got some dead and some wounded. And . . . ah . . ."

"What else?"

"A lot of the yeller-bellied cowpokes who kinda sympathized with the Wests have snuck out and left us. The cook's stove is dented to pieces, and the foodstuff is shot up. The cook quit, and now the boys are mad as wet prairie chickens at the idea of no grub."

"Forget that for a minute," said Poindexter. "Kid Kurt was here, and he left on the train to Denver. I bet he's going to hire men. We've got some planning to do."

"Yes, Boss?"

"I want you to send a couple trackers—those Indians we kept back at the old line shack—to eliminate those snipers. Then, I want a rider to go after those gun-hands I hired. You know where they're at. I want every man who can tote a gun to be here within two days. Then send telegrams across the territory that we're hiring gun slicks. We'll have this town covered from one end to the other. When that West kid returns with men, we'll wipe them out. Then we'll take care of their ranch. I've got something to teach that Priscilla West, and the lessons long overdue."

"Is that it, Boss?"

"Isn't that enough?"

"Sure, Boss. Only we was all wondering about food and a cook."

"Why did you let the cook leave? Should've held a gun

to his head."

"You've got to be kidding. With a salty cook like him, we're liable to end up poisoned."

"Well, go wake up Ramsey at the restaurant and take him with you. He owes me. Tell him I sent you."

"Right, Boss. Might satisfy the boys a bit. Be back in a couple days loaded for bear."

Poindexter paced the room.

Here I sit on thousands of acres of land, practically own everything in town, and those blasted Wests are still interfering in my plans. How is it possible for a handful of people to continue to defy me? I'll get them this time. I'll stomp them into the ground, and there won't be anything left. That goes for that nosy doctor, his wife, and that priest.

CHAPTER TWENTY-SIX

The territorial governor and the chief from the U.S. Marshall Service sat together in the governor's office and discussed the growing pile of letters from Dr. Bennett; his new wife, and the priest, Father Torres. This latest about John West being bushwhacked on Wet Springs Ranch certainly seemed to show an escalation in hostilities between the local citizens and this Poindexter.

"If you want to be elected governor again, you will have to do something," said the U.S. Marshall.

"It's beginning to look that way," responded the governor.

"Look, they write that they're forming a vigilante committee. They say Poindexter keeps on hiring gun-hands and the crooked sheriff supports him. They want a U.S. Marshall to come down and enforce the law."

"What do you suggest?" asked the governor.

"Give me two of your special deputies, and we'll go."

CHAPTER TWENTY-SEVEN

"Has it been three days or just two since this started?" Jedidiah Taylor murmured out loud to himself.

Maybe I am getting a little old for this kind of thing, he thought. *Ain't been hardly no movement now. Can't be sure at night, though. Gotta git me some sleep. Wonder how many I got? Wounded some, too. Shot the heck out of those bunkhouses and the cook shack. I bet Poindexter's gunslingers went loco when they found thar weren't no grub. Wonder if I persuaded them varmints to quit? What's that sound? Gettin awful jumpy now. Guess I shouldn't have been so pigheaded. Could have used one more person up here. Still, I got this here job to do.*

It was dusk of the third day when Jedidiah saw movement off to the east. He pulled up the Sharps and fired. From behind came two Indians. One scraped his moccasins on the granite rock. Jedidiah turned halfway just as the two trackers shot him in the back. The mountain man went down. The two waited and saw no movement. They noted it was just an old man. The first Indian pushed Jedidiah's shoulder. The mountain man, using the last of his strength, drove his Bowie knife into the Indian's chest and he felt it go through and scrape the spine. Jedidiah Taylor drew his six-gun and shot the other Indian in the head. The old mountain man sank backwards onto the ground, the weight of the first dead Indian upon him.

My old pards would have been proud of this one, he thought and, despite it still being light out, darkness came to his open eyes.

CHAPTER TWENTY-EIGHT

Dr. Bennett, his wife, Father Torres, Juan, Carmen, and Rosa sat around the big kitchen table at Wet Springs.

"What are we to do?" asked Juan looking first at Father Torres and then at Dr. Bennett. "The Wests have been very good to us. We cannot let Mrs. West and Kurt down right now. We must defend Wet Springs."

"That is a brave commitment, Juan," said Dr. Bennett. "Protecting it won't be easy."

"Si," continued Father Torres. "Word has come to me that Kurt has gone to Denver to hire men who are skilled with guns. Poindexter is doing the same. It has been a long time coming, but the big conflict is here. Señora West must be protected."

"I agree," answered the doctor. "But how?"

"My people tell me," said Father Torres, "that someone is shooting up Poindexter's ranch, and he is very angry."

"Jedidiah has been gone a long time," said Juan.

"Too long," returned Dr. Bennett. "You don't suppose he is the one shooting, do you?"

"I think it is Jedidiah," Juan replied. "Who else, but him?"

"We must bury Señor West," said Carmen. "We cannot wait for Kurt and the others to return."

"Yes," answered the priest. "Señora West is too ill to make decisions. Do you have any thoughts as to where?"

"I hear Señor John West talk about how beautiful it is at the canyon," said Carmen.

"Si," Juan agreed. "He would go there often when he had much on his mind."

"Then we will bury him there," said Father Torres. "We can have a fitting memorial service later."

Even though the mourners were few and the words short, the grief was heartfelt as the little group of friends carried John West's body to the place where he had last walked. They buried him beneath the cliff of rock by the canyon gate.

Father Torres and Dr. Bennett left for town and his wife, Kate, stayed to care for Priscilla. On the way, the two men talked about organizing people against Poindexter. They must be ready to defend Red Wing.

"I never thought I would ever be part of a vigilante committee, much less help organize one," said the doctor.

"Nor I," answered the priest. "But we seem to have no choice. We cannot have more innocent people killed. God forgive us."

CHAPTER TWENTY-NINE

After Kurt and his men finished their meal, he asked them to separate and spread the word in stores, saloons, and other businesses that Wet Springs Ranch was hiring. They would be interviewing at the hotel in the morning. They must be of good character and able to use guns.

The sheriff's office was where Kurt went first. A rather stern gentleman in a frocked coat met him. He wore a badge on his lapel, and a long-barreled pistol on his hip.

"What can I help you with?"

Kurt explained.

"What might your name be?

"Kurt West."

"From?"

"Red Wing is the nearest town, and our ranch is called Wet Springs."

"Is that down near Walsenburg?"

"Yes, sir, some twenty miles east of Wet Springs."

"Seems I heard there was a might of trouble down there. The governor himself told me."

"Are you going to help me or not?"

"Not before I ask what side you're on, son."

"My names Kurt, and I'm on the right side. Men killed my father, and we need help against a poisonous snake called Poindexter."

"Now that's the name I heard! Seems local people are writing the governor about him."

"Good. I hope they're telling the truth. Poindexter is nothing but a land grabber and hires men to do his killing."

"I might know of a couple good men. I'll send them over in the morning."

"Thank you, Sir," said Kurt. "You know my name, could I know yours?" The Sheriff looked at Kurt in surprise and extending his hand, smiled. "They call me, David J. Cook, Sheriff Arapahoe County."

The young gunfighter nodded and shook hands. Both men kept eye contact, and the younger man did not return the smile.

Kurt left and began walking the town, informing men of his intent and vaguely taking in the sights. He went back to the hotel and into the saloon. A variety show was on stage with dance hall girls in bright dresses. The main attraction was a female singer. Kurt watched a while and sipped on a cup of coffee. Then he went upstairs to his room to sleep.

The sun was barely up when Kurt awoke. He dressed and went straight to a gunsmith shop and banged on the door. He purchased two .50 caliber Sharps with scopes and five hundred rounds of ammunition. An order for pistols was made, new or used didn't matter as long as they fired well. He asked for a large amount of ammunition for them, along with rifles. Kurt found out where he could buy horses and went and inspected the animals. He picked out eight.

He made a fair offer and was rejected. He started to walk away, and the man called him back and made the deal.

Returning to the hotel, he met his companions for breakfast. It looked like Shorty had taken one too many nips at the red-eye the night before. After breakfast they went to the lobby, and the clerk directed them to two private rooms. One was large with many chairs, and the other was small and had just five as requested. In the larger room, sitting in one of the chairs, was an old man. He looked a lot like Jedidiah. The Wet Springs crew went to the small back room and sat down. Kurt asked Issy to conduct the man in.

"Well, they said you were hiring, so here's I am," said the old westerner.

"How come you're the only one out there?" asked Kurt. "Aren't any more coming?"

"Hell's fire, boy, after what was spread around town yesterday, you'll have every busted and broken-down kind of a feller in here before dark. That thar room out thar is going to be plumb chuck full every kind of runt. I'm here first cause I'm the only one in town gets out of bed this early."

"Tell us about yourself," asked Kurt.

"I can yell like a banshee, drink like a fish, swim the Pecos when it's dry, cook my own grub—and eat it, and still be alive. Heck, boy, tell me what you want, and I'll give it to you."

"Quit calling me boy unless you want to leave. Can you shoot?"

"If'n I couldn't, I wouldn't be alive right now. I heard

about you, Kid, and that's why I'm here. In the old days, I shot a Spencer at them buffalo. I know the Sharps .50; I can use a Bowie and every kind of six-gun. I'm partial to the long gun. I've been all over the west and done stuff too numerous to brag on. Haw! It ain't my fault I lived this long and I'm still alive."

Kurt looked to his men. They nodded their heads.

"What's your name, old-timer?"

"Call me by my rightful handle—Griz. Haw! Haw!"

"Alright Griz, you're going shopping. Here's twenty dollars. Go buy yourself a new outfit and report back here. I already ordered you a Sharps with a scope and a horse. And Griz?"

"Yeah?"

"Do us all a favor, and take a bath before you put on the new duds."

"You mean, on the outside?"

"Yes. You know, with soap and water?"

"What is this, a social club?"

"No," said Shorty. "But we like our partners to smell tolerable."

"Got me thar! Haw! Haw!"

By noon the room was overfull, and men were pushing each other. The place reeked of unwashed bodies. The hotel manager came in and complained. So far, out of the many interviews, they only managed to hire the old man. He hadn't returned. Most of the men seemed to be thugs or derelicts.

There came a loud crash from outside. The four clambered to the door and saw a small Chinese man using his hands, feet, and arms in a fight against two rough-looking characters. Two men were out cold on the floor. Kurt yelled for order and the fighting stopped. They brought the little man into the back room and closed the door.

"What was that about?" asked Kurt.

"Four ruffians thought to take advantage of Wong Lee. They not succeed." All this in perfect English from a man dressed head to foot in traditional Chinese working clothes.

"You speak English very well."

"Yes, I am well educated in China, and also I carry dictionary with me." Wong Lee mysteriously pulled a small book from his clothing.

"What can you do for us, Wong Lee?"

"I can do innumerable things—too many to mention, but as you see, I am first-class fighting man. Do I get the job?"

"Wait. First explain how or why you are here, and why you would want to leave your people to come work for us."

"In China, I killed an official. He was a bad man. But it means death. So I escape to here. Now I offer my services."

"Do you know how to ride?"

"Yes, I learn in China."

"Do you know how to shoot a pistol? A rifle?"

"No, but I learn."

"I'm sorry, Wong Lee, but you would be very lonely away from your people, and we don't have time to teach you to shoot."

"I work very hard for Kid Kurt and his family. You give

me little bit of land, and I send for mail-order bride, make babies, and live happily. Besides, I have other skills."

Wong Lee produced two strange-looking knives from his clothing and spun them across the room into the wall above the heads of Shorty and Carlos. With an imperceptible movement, two more appeared and he flung them directly beside the other two.

Kurt's eyes widened, and a slow grin spread across his face.

"I also can shoot bow and arrow better. These I can do now—with no training. You need a man who can kill silently."

Kurt looked at the others, and they nodded.

"Okay, Wong Lee, you are hired. Here is twenty dollars. I want you to buy western clothes. It won't do to walk around with what you're wearing. Fetch all the knives you have and bring a bow and arrows. If you need more money, come back, but be here before dark."

"Yes, Wong Lee will come back a cowboy, and no one will know I am Chinese. You think so?"

After the door closed, Kurt turned to his men. "Two down. Six to go."

"Seems that you're starting out with some mighty strange hands, partner," said Shorty.

"If this keeps up, we'll stand out for sure," added Issy.

They interviewed through lunchtime and had food brought to them. Every man they interviewed was unsuitable. Two men arrived who were tight-faced and silent. Kurt asked questions, but they remained reticent. Finally, they got around to saying they worked for the sheriff as occasional lawmen. They asked to be given a chance. That was good enough endorsement for Kurt. They gave their names as Bill Banks and Tom Williams.

Another fight began in the waiting room, and the Wet Springs crew went out to break it up. Chairs were being broken over men's heads. The hotel manager barged in and demanded the rooms be cleared and damages be paid. A figure was mentioned, and Kurt handed over the money.

"Now what are we going to do, Señor Kurt?" asked Carlos.

They went to the restaurant and had coffee. Later, in their rooms, they waited for the hired men. Griz showed up in a new outfit, looking and smelling cleaner. Bill and Tom returned with rifles and gear. Wong Lee showed up, and he was grinning from ear to ear. His outfit was splashy, but he looked good. He carried a bow and two quivers full of arrows. Under his vest, he had strapped on rows of throwing knives in a wide leather belt.

A knock on the door was heard. Kurt opened it, and a young man about his own age came into the crowded hotel room.

"You the gent that's hiring?" asked the young cowboy. "Can I talk to you about it?"

"Go ahead," said Kurt.

"Here? In front of everyone?"

"Yes."

"Me and my pards are looking to go straight. I mean to find a way to make a living the honest way. We was all brought up right, but when we got out here, there were no decent jobs. We had to eat. We heard you wanted someone who would fight. There's four of us. My names Spider, and my pards are Jack, Sam, and Buster.

"Where did you learn to shoot?" asked Shorty.

"We've been practicing," answered Spider.

"Where're your friends?" asked Kurt.

"Hidden out," replied Spider. "They said I was wasting my time."

"We know these boys," said Bill Banks, former deputy. "A little stealing and rustling. They never hurt good folk."

A month back, I was in an outlaw cantina," added Tom Williams, the other deputy. "Five men braced these boys. Tough hombres. Only one of them toughs lived to talk about it. I reckon they are good men to have in a fight."

"Here's eighty dollars, Spider, twenty apiece for each of you to buy new outfits. You and your friends meet me here before dark."

"They said it was no good comin here, but I heard you were square," said Spider. "Thanks."

"I expect the best from you," said Kurt. "Buy what you need. Meet in the morning, early. We'll get acquainted and do a little gun practice outside of town."

In the morning the Wet Springs crew, with their new hired hands, met in front of the hotel and went to a local restaurant. Kurt paid for breakfast. Gathering at the stables, he furnished horses and gear for those down on their luck. They rode several miles north and out of town. As arranged, the gunsmith and a wagon with supplies were waiting. Targets, empty bottles, and barrels were set up at various distances.

"Alright," said Kurt. "If we're going to risk our lives against Poindexter's men, then every man here has the right to know what the other person next to him can do. I'll go first."

Smoothly, but with precision and speed, Kurt drew his right-hand pistol and, fanning the hammer, a row of five whiskey bottles shattered and fell. He opened the chamber, withdrew the empties, and reloaded.

"You're next, Shorty."

Shorty stepped up and drew both pistols at once and shot first with the right and next with the left, destroying five more bottles. Shorty punched out his empties and reloaded.

"Who's next?"

Wong Lee came forward and with blinding speed threw six knives at the center of one barrel. They landed with terrific force and within a space of the width of a man's hand. Next, he took the bow and nocked an arrow. The arrow pierced the target dead center at twenty-five yards. He nocked another arrow and let fly. This one over a hundred feet away. The arrow flew in a curved arch and hit very near the center of the target. A murmur of approval went around the group.

"Who's next?"

Bill Banks and Tom Williams both stepped up and asked for more bottles. They seemed to do everything together. They drew and aimed; Bill shot six bottles on the left and Tom, six on the right. They both stepped back.

"Next," called Kurt.

Spider, his partner Jack, and Sam shot their pistols.

Each hit their target. They did the same with rifles. Buster, a strange, gawky-looking boy with glasses, made the comment that he couldn't hit a thing with a pistol or a rifle. He carried two cut down, double-barreled, Greener shotguns in leather holsters. He fired the left and then the right, partially destroying the twenty-five-yard paper target.

Next came Griz who pulled a Bowie knife and hit dead center at a barrel. Then he picked up a .50 caliber Sharps. He shot three times at a tree some five hundred yards away.

"One of you ride out and see what he hit," asked Kurt.

Issy jumped on a horse, rode out and examined the tree. Returning, he said, "He's gonna give Jedidiah some competition."

"I think it's agreed, we can count on each other," said Kurt. "Shorty, I want you to try to teach Wong Lee how to use a rifle. The rest of you can shoot or do whatever you want."

For an hour, the plains thundered with sounds of gunfire. It was nearly noon, and Kurt suggested they take a break for lunch. No sooner had he spoken when a very shabbily dressed young man came walking up out of a wash.

"Please, señores, I wish to speak to those who are hiring men."

"You're too late," said Kurt, looking the poor fellow over.

"Please, Señor Kurt. You give me a chance, por favor. I show you I can shoot and defend your ranch."

The young man pulled back his serape and revealed a battered holster and an ancient pistol. He bent down, picked up a small stone, threw it high into the air, drew and fired. The rock shattered.

"Alright, so you can shoot," said Kurt. "Now tell us why you meet us out here."

The Wet Springs crew stood around quietly studying the exchange.

"I know you. My people, they talk of you. You are Señor Kid Kurt, and you have the Wet Springs Ranch where workers are treated fairly. Señor Kurt, I wish to join you. I don't speak just for myself."

The young man whistled and a small but very pretty young woman came from the gully. She was holding a baby.

"I am sorry, Señor..." said Kurt. "But..."

"I am Ramone. Please call me Ramone."

"I am sorry, Ramone, but we can't take your wife and baby with us. It would be too dangerous."

"You don't understand, Señor! It is too dangerous for us to stay here. You see, that is my sister, Consuelo. Two white men of the town see her coming home from work and—well—they hurt her. Then the baby comes. I go to the sheriff, and he tells me to go away. He will not listen to me since one of the men who hurt Consuelo is important man. So I go to the men and tell them there is a baby, and they beat me."

"Please Ramone, I don't think..."

"So I buy this gun with the little money I have, and I work, and I save, and I buy ammunition. Still, my money is not enough. But, I shoot, I practice, I buy bullets instead of food. I am hungry, but I learn. I go to these men, and

I call them out in the street just like the white men do. They laugh…it is two against the little Mexican Ramone. They draw, and I shoot them for my sister, for the baby, for justice, and for me to feel like a man again."

There was complete silence now as the Wet Springs crew leaned forward to hear every word. Even Kurt listened intently.

"The sheriff and many men chase me. But, I hide and they not find me. Am I not allowed to defend my sister and her honor? I do nothing wrong. It is because Consuelo and I are Mexican. You understand, Señor Kurt, we cannot stay here. We need your help. If you let us come with you, we both work very hard. You can trust us. We will defend you and your ranch."

"If you let him talk any longer," complained Shorty, "you'll have us bawlin' wors'en a herd of cows. For land's sake, hire the man and let's get some grub."

The cowboys looked over at Consuelo and saw Wong Lee standing beside her. He had the baby in his arms and was smiling at the girl.

"I don't want any trouble from you, Ramone, about that; Wong Lee is part of our crew now."

"No trouble, Señor," said Ramone, nodding his head in understanding. "Only God can determine what good comes to my sister and her baby."

Kurt looked around the circle at his other hands, and they nodded their heads.

"Alright, Ramone, you and your sister and her baby are with us now."

"Muchas gracias, Señor Kurt. You will not regret this."

"Carlos and Issy, ride into town and bring back a couple of new outfits for the girl and Ramone. Ask the lady what she needs for the baby. We can get other things for them later. Purchase two more horses and saddles and bring that stuff back here."

"The gunsmith has brought food in his wagon, I'm starved," said Shorty.

So, what had been a group of twelve was now fifteen—including an unmarried mother and a little baby.

In the morning Kurt settled up with the hotel, and the entire crew loaded the horses onto a boxcar. Food, water, ammunition, guns, and all the gear were loaded onto a second boxcar in which Kurt and his crew would ride. They had arranged with the railroad that it would stop at the stockyards and let them off before going into town.

CHAPTER THIRTY

Penelope Hathaway got on the train in Maryland and started her arduous journey home. How she missed the West, the dry climate, and the wide-open sky. There, in the clear air, the scenery extended out as far as the eye could see. Nothing was like it in the East and never would be. Everything was so pure, so elemental, so natural, so majestic in the West. She hated the East with its false tameness, its rules and laws that only increased the power of those with money and position. The so-called civilization and its large cities merely gave an illusion of civility. Lurking underneath was untamed brutality, trickery, and deceit. The people of the East lived narrow little lives. They knew nothing of the wide-open freedom of the American West.

How many immature and spoiled Eastern boys had accosted her? She handled them easily except for two. One, a rich boy, told everyone at a dance that he was going to marry her and tame the West out of her. She had slapped his face and shouted at him loud enough for the entire room to hear. No, she wasn't going to marry a rich, spoiled, egotistical boy under any circumstances. He got the message, and she had made an enemy for life.

The other young man was not so easily handled. It was Penelope's great beauty and aloof coldness that drove such men on. This other suitor was devious, arrogant, and relentless, and much more dangerous. He rumored it about that one way or the other he would have her. He stalked her; he seemed to be everywhere. He tried to wear her down with gifts and intrigue. In every way possible she rebuffed this cad, but it did no good. Then, he resorted to plots of kidnapping, of attempting to whisk her away to a remote house in the country. To this end, he paid some of her friends who thought they were assisting with a jest; he also paid some of her enemies. One night a young lady friend of Penelope's led her into a carriage in which the cad was hiding. He grabbed Penelope and attempted to tie her up. Penelope drew out a very sharp dagger and stabbed him in the leg. Horrified, he shouted from the pain of the deep wound and profuse bleeding. The other girl screamed, and Penelope menacingly told her to shut up. She held the dagger against her abductor and whispered to him.

"If you don't stop this carriage instantly, I will cut you!"

"You stabbed me!"

"And I will do it again. Did you think this was a game to abduct me and suffer no consequences? Come near me again, and I will kill you."

The carriage stopped, and Penelope got down and walked away from her tearful female acquaintance who kept begging forgiveness.

"Wait, Penelope, please don't be angry," called the young woman. "It was only a joke."

"You are a shallow and simpleminded fool. You put me

in danger, and call it a lark? Never talk to me again."

Penelope left the East, knowing that she did not want to return. And yet, she appreciated that her schooling had been excellent, and many of her instructors were people who had challenged and enlightened her. She had gained an education that would help her throughout her life.

Sitting there in the train coach, Penelope turned her thoughts to home, to her mother, and to Kurt. She was getting close. In Denver, it looked like they added two cattle cars to the back. Must be taking empties back to pick up a shipment of cattle, she thought.

In the past four years she had written Kurt many times. He responded to each letter but sometimes only wrote a card and a few short words. Penelope read and reread them, looking for signs that he loved her. He wrote that he did, but still, he had not given her the assurance she really wanted. How many times had she relived the days on Promontory Point and the sweet smell of sunshine baking the dusty earth. She remembered the wind playing in his hair and the blue of the sky mirroring the blue of his eyes.

Does he remember the dance? How we kissed and held hands? Will he still like the way I look now that I am eighteen and a woman? People back East said I was a beauty, a desert flower. Will Kurt think so? Does he think about me at all? Will he still look the same? So sweet, so strong, yet so kind and exciting? Maybe he will no longer like me. Perhaps it was merely a childish romance.

"Darn, I hate this riding and waiting," she said out loud. *I cannot wait to see mother. I wonder why she hasn't been writing much lately. I can't imagine why unless she is ill or that horrid stepfather of mine has done something to hinder her letters.*

The train slowed down and stopped. Outside, near some pens, the noise of horses moving about came to her ears.

Now that's the real West, she thought to herself. *All those years back east have made me soft. I should have packed my pistol.*

CHAPTER THIRTY-ONE

Alone in his office at the back of the saloon, Poindexter strapped on a pair of matched, gold inlaid .45 caliber pistols. The leather holsters were hand-carved. Yes, he could shoot better than most; for years he had practiced with a gun, even when he had lived in the East and worked for his wife's first husband. He could fight, too. He often worked out in his private quarters.

Everything he did, he did with a purpose and a vengeance. Secretly and behind the scenes was the way he preferred it. Why let anyone know he could shoot? Why let anyone know he could fight? Let them think he was a coward. Let them think he stood behind others and that he was a weakling. Then, if he must, and only if absolutely necessary, would he act on his own behalf to defend what was his, including his own life.

Didn't the ruse of not being a gun-toter save my life twice? He laughed out loud to himself. *I lived, didn't I? Only time I came close to giving myself away was when that West woman backhanded me in the church. I hate that woman, and she's going to pay. It took all the willpower I could muster not to break her neck. But, people around here who know what's good for them, know I have the guts to act. I don't give a darn what others think.*

Billings cautiously knocked at the outer door of the office. Poindexter's foreman still had a bruise from the paperweight.

"Come in."

"Boss, we got the men stationed on the roofs throughout town. Just like you said. Say," said Billings, eyeing the pistols Poindexter was wearing. "I didn't know you could shoot."

"There's a lot you don't know, and we'll keep it that way. The men have plenty of ammunition for those rifles?"

"Yes, like you said, fifty rounds each."

"How many men do we have?"

"Sixteen on the roofs, ten stationed at either end of town, seven in the buildings on the north, and eight on the south. Here in the saloon, we have five counting you and me."

"I asked you how many men altogether."

"Forty-six counting the both of us."

"Good, that should do it. I want them on guard for as long as it takes. I want you to figure out shifts for sleeping and eating. Everyone stays at their posts. You understand this?"

"Yes, Boss, I do. The boys won't like it none, but they'll stay put."

"Did you get any answer to my telegrams for more gun-hands?"

"No, Boss. No telegrams and no one has shown up to collect the fifty dollars. Sure seems strange. Thought they'd come in droves."

"I'm going down to the telegraph office and see what's going on. Maybe the darn line is down somewhere. Then I'll meet the train. It's due in half an hour. I'll see if anyone special gets off. You take care of the fort. I hold you responsible for everything, Billings. Understand?"

"Yes, sir, Boss."

Poindexter walked into the little telegraph office inside the railroad station. The operator, sitting in his cubbyhole, was sending out a message. The little man stopped when Poindexter thumped the counter and yelled.

"Where's the answer to my telegrams, you sawed-off ticker-tapper?"

"M-M-M-Mr. P-P-P-Poindexter, sir, I keep sending them out, like I did just now. The other end says message confirmed and received—but then nothing. It's like someone is standing there pulling them before they're delivered."

"Has anything like this happened before?" Poindexter asked, thinking he may have a bigger problem.

"No, sir, never. It would take someone pretty important."

Poindexter walked away, turning this development over in his mind. *Could the government be involved? No. I am the government around here. Who would take an interest in me?*

Poindexter stepped outside and onto the platform. In the distance, the whistle blew, and several people stood around waiting to see what the train brought. The train's arrival was daily entertainment for many folks as well as a break from their dull and routine life.

With a scream of breaks, hissing steam, and black smoke, the iron beast rumbled to a stop near the platform. Several men got out and proceeded to assist a very beautiful young lady down the steps. She wore a fashionable dress and hat. Her hair was long and light brown, almost blond. She had a marvelous figure. Poindexter stared. He ate her up with his eyes. Somehow this woman seemed familiar.

Two men, along with the conductor and a baggage man with a little pull cart, went to collect her baggage. An enormous amount of luggage was piled on the cart and, when that was full, the rest was stacked on the platform. Poindexter sauntered down near the activity and listened intently.

"Someone be here to pick you up, Miss?" asked the porter as he lifted her last trunk onto the cart.

"I am certain there will be. I mailed a letter to my mother weeks ago. She must be running late."

He hadn't recognized the face, but he knew the voice instantly. "Unbelievable," murmured Poindexter to himself. "Penelope. My, my, my. How little girls do grow up."

Poindexter frowned and thought about his wife. The reason his wife hadn't received the letter was because for the last six weeks she had been locked in her room.

That woman dared to defy me, he thought. *I gave her a good beating and locked her up. I enjoyed that. Good thing the house is built solidly. Hmm, I didn't read that letter. It must lay somewhere back on my desk. Perhaps a change in plans is in order,* he thought. *I can use a little recreation.*

Poindexter stepped towards the beautiful young woman. "Excuse me. Penelope, I presume?"

She turned around in excitement, then frowned when she saw who had spoken.

I'll wipe that frown off her face when she gets home, thought Poindexter angrily.

"So it's you. Where is Mother?"

"She's at home. She's not feeling well and sent me to fetch you."

"What is wrong with her? Should we get the doctor to go with us?"

"No, no. She fell down the stairs a few weeks ago, and she's recovering. She's bedridden, but on the mend. Listen, I'll get a buggy and return, should only take about fifteen minutes."

"Please hurry. I want to see Mother right away. Now that I'm here, I'll take care of her."

Poindexter couldn't wipe the smirk from his face. *She'll take care of someone all right, but it won't be her mother.*

At the saloon, he ordered Billings to go get a large buggy and make sure it had space for the luggage.

"Boss, we found out who did the shooting. It was that old mountain man, Jedidiah. One of my men checked. Found him and the two Indians dead up in that jumble of rocks."

"Well, that's something," said Poindexter. "Now go get me that buggy."

The big foreman did as directed and came back with the conveyance and two matched horses.

"Billings, I changed my mind. Just for tonight I'll be

spending time at the ranch. My orders stand the way I gave them. Make sure you carry them out."

"Yes, sir, Boss. I will."

Poindexter drove the vehicle up to the loading dock, and the porter stacked the luggage. The train had already pulled out. Penelope was helped up onto the seat.

The Poindexter ranch was several hours away. The road was quite bumpy, but Penelope's thoughts were focused on her mother. Poindexter was strangely silent except to ask her about that pistol she always carried. Absentmindedly, she remarked she was out of the habit due to living in the East. Poindexter smiled.

They pulled up in front of the enormous house, and Poindexter helped Penelope down. She loathed this man, and her skin crawled when he touched her, but she tried not to let it show. Penelope ran to the massive double doors and pulled one open. She hurried through the tiled foyer into a large room with marble floors, Persian rugs, chandeliers, and a wide stairway. Penelope was blind to the grandeur and flew up the stairs as fast as she could go. She raced to her mother's room and turned the door handle. The door was locked! She spun around to confront Poindexter, who was right behind her. Before Penelope could say anything, he produced a large skeleton key for the thick oak door

"For her own protection I keep the room locked," he said as he turned the key. "Go and see your mother. Then come back and tell me what you think."

With great dread and a churning feeling in her stomach, Penelope entered the stuffy room. It was dark with the heavy curtains shut. She threw them back in order to see, and she tried to open a window. It was nailed closed. The room smelled of someone shut in for days with no one to change the bedpan.

Penelope saw her mother lying in bed. She was frail and emaciated. She had aged horribly. Her face was wrinkled, and there were large streaks of gray in her hair. There was a bottle of water near the bed on a stand. Penelope tasted it and then gently touched her mother whose eyes were closed and tried to get her to awaken and take a drink. After some time, she succeeded.

She's dying, thought the girl fighting tears. *He's done this to her. If he comes near her again, I'll kill him. I may not have my pistol, but I still have the dagger, and I'll cut his liver out. That swine is going to pay.*

"Penelope." her mother said weakly. "Oh, Penelope, I almost gave up hope. Quick, Penelope, we must escape. You don't know what a monster he is. You are in great danger."

"A little late for that warning, my dear," said Poindexter, who had slipped into the room unnoticed.

"What have you done to my mother? She's nearly dead!"

"If you only knew half of it, you'd really be angry." He smirked, his words matching his venomous tone.

"You slimy creature. Get out of here. Mother and I are leaving whether you like it or not."

"Afraid that's not possible, Penelope, honey. That's not at all what I have in mind for you. No, my dear spunky stepdaughter, not at all. I am extremely delighted to have you home." Poindexter's eyes narrowed as he lasciviously leered at Penelope.

"Poindexter, you are a spineless worm! What hold do you have over my mother?"

"My, such language from a lady. Is that any way to speak to your adoring stepfather? After all, didn't I just pay for you to attend the most prestigious school in the East? Shame on you," he crooned, his eyes moving over her.

"Pig!" Penelope growled. Her expression changed from anger to pain as she saw her mother cringe as if in agony. "What has he done to you? What does he mean by it is impossible for us to leave? What hold has he on you? I've known for years that you don't love this man."

"How observant, my dear." Poindexter's expression changed to one of contempt as he looked first at his wife and then back at Penelope. "All right, if you insist. I'll tell you why your mother married me."

"Poindexter, no!" screamed Cynthia. "You promised on your life to never tell. You can't, not to my own daughter!"

"I can't? My dear, I can do anything I like. And, since you're never leaving this room again, I will tell it as it really happened."

"Please, if there is any decency left in you," pleaded Cynthia, "don't do this."

"Quit begging," snarled Poindexter. "Listen carefully, Penelope, and if you don't want to see your mother hurt, I suggest you sit there and keep your pretty mouth shut. It is time for your history lesson."

Penelope started to speak and then closed her mouth.

"Your mother was married to your father, Glenn

Hathaway, a rich man, an active man, a pillar of the community, a lawyer. I worked in one of his offices, and fortune was with me. I worked my way up to become one of his private secretaries. I had access to his public as well as his private life. I hated the man, but he never suspected it. He was righteous and benevolent. He went to church and gave to charities and strongly encouraged his employees to do the same. He was powerful, and it made me sick. I saw him for what he was—a fool—a man wasting his life and his money."

Poindexter paced the floor as he talked, all the while keeping his eyes closely locked on Penelope's face, thrilled at her amazed attention.

"I devised a plan to take over everything. I hired a beautiful woman to work in his office. She pretended to be my secretary. The fool didn't even notice her even though she exuded her trade. So I planted notes, love notes, between the blond secretary and your father. Your mother read them and became jealous. I fueled that jealousy until it reached a fevered pitch. I arranged a business meeting in the office after hours. The blond secretary was there; your father was there bending over the desk looking at important papers, and she was beside him. I was near the door when Cynthia burst in. It took a lot of bribing, but following my instructions, the blond grabbed Glenn Hathaway and kissed him."

"No! No more, Poindexter! Give me a gun, and I'll shoot myself! I can't bear to hear any more!" screamed Cynthia as she lurched to a sitting position. "For my sake, don't tell Penelope what I did."

Poindexter stepped near the bed, barely missing his wife's claw-like grasp, amazed at the strength the emaciated woman exhibited.

"A gun? For you to shoot yourself? Yes, that could be arranged. In fact, that would be quite convenient, but I do believe you are worth more to me alive. Am I right, Penelope?" he laughed as he watched her reaction.

"Now that I have your attention, for the first time, both of you will hear what really happened. You see Cynthia, my dearest, all this time you thought you were the one who did it. You, poor, gullible fool. You're no different than he was. All these years I've despised you."

"Please," whispered Cynthia Poindexter, "please stop."

"Do you want to hear what really happened? You pulled your pistol from your purse and in a fit of jealous rage shot at the secretary and your husband. Then you fainted. What you never knew, my wife, is that you couldn't even do that right. You shot four times and you missed. I picked up your gun and shot your husband in the head, and then I shot the blond in the chest. I put the gun in your husband's hand to make it look like a murder-suicide. You, I carried out and took home. I convinced you that you had killed them both and that the only thing to do was let the authorities investigate."

"You fiend!" hissed Cynthia.

"So you let them interview you, and they exonerated you. As quickly as we could, we sold the business, took the money, little Penelope, and ran west. I convinced you to let me take you somewhere no one knew you and, for your sake," he said nodding at Penelope, "escape the crime. And, that's what we did. With the money we started with, I have doubled—no—tripled the amount. Now, who is the better man?"

"You filthy monster!" shouted Cynthia. "All these years you have let me condemn myself, and I am innocent. Thank God, I didn't kill Glenn."

"Oh yes, you are technically innocent. But you would have killed him had you not been such a poor shot. I simply did the job for you. You are still guilty, my dear."

"Why have you told us this now?" asked Penelope.

"Why, this is my home. I am the man of the house, and I take my privileges as I see them. I have invested in your education, and now you have come back to reward me."

Poindexter drew a gun and pointed it at his wife.

"Penelope, get out into the hallway if you value your mother's life."

"Penelope, don't listen to the monster," Cynthia sobbed.

Penelope did as she was told, and clung to her only hope, the hidden dagger. She watched as Poindexter locked her mother's room. He then put the pistol away and, grinning lustily, grabbed Penelope. She was shocked. This man had hands of iron and muscles of steel, and she was helpless. He dragged her into his bedroom and slammed the door shut with his foot. He reached up to the neckline of her dress and with one tremendous heave ripped half her dress off. He picked her up and, laughing, threw her down onto his large bed. She landed and bounced. She reached under her dress and grabbed the dagger from its scabbard. She held it up. It was her mistake. Poindexter laughed again. His right hand darted out and he grabbed her wrist in a vice-like grip. The knife fell on the bed and then onto the floor. He forced her down on the bed, and his mouth came down on hers. He tasted like the foul thing he was.

An explosion sounded in the outside hallway—then another. A thump and then Poindexter's door banged open. Into the room staggered Cynthia Poindexter, holding a pistol in both hands. Poindexter stopped what he was doing and looked at his wife. He burst into derisive laughter.

"Cynthia, you couldn't shoot anything back then, what makes you think you can hit anything now?"

"You vile, snake. You most despicable human being. You don't know anything about me. You never have. Get up."

Poindexter, still laughing and sure of his advantage over this frail woman, rose and stood before his wife, who was perhaps twenty feet away. He smirked as he began to draw his revolver. Cynthia fired and shot him in the right shoulder. Poindexter, startled and in pain, continued drawing his pistol. Before he could fire, Cynthia shot him in the left shoulder. His revolver dropped

"Now, walk out of this room," ordered Cynthia, her confidence increasing. "Get down that stairway, and out of this house."

Painfully, blood flowing from both wounds, Poindexter stepped toward his wife. Cynthia backed away from him and stopped at the top of the stairs. Penelope jumped up from the bed and attempted to grab the bleeding man. Then Poindexter made a headlong dive to push his wife down the stairs. Cynthia fired a third time, and the bullet took Poindexter full in the chest. He fell, and his momentum rolled him down the stairs. He lay in a heap at the bottom—

bleeding profusely—his breath coming in great gasps.

"No! This can't be! Not after all I worked for! Cynthia? How?" His words were barely audible to the two women at the top of the stairs.

"All these years in the West and you didn't think I would learn to shoot?" said the wife. "I've been practicing, Mr. Poindexter. I've been practicing."

The evil man who had caused so many deaths and so much pain took one great breath, shuddered, and died.

Cynthia, weakened by her efforts, sagged into her daughter's arms. From the top of the stairs, she looked down at the dead man at the bottom, and for the first time in years, she smiled.

CHAPTER THIRTY-TWO

Kurt sat on the clean straw of the boxcar and wondered if he should have left Tiger in the care of Issy's friends. How he loved that furry little beast and his horse, Cindy. It was if they were extensions of himself. He thought about the incredible courage and instinct they both had that made them rush into the saloon. It was too remarkable to believe, but it had happened. He was still alive.

Kurt looked around at his crew—twelve men, the girl, and her baby. In a few short hours, they would be on their horses heading for town. Who will live and who will die? He felt the weight of the responsibility of other people's lives upon his shoulders.

I am too young for this. What right do I have to ask men to fight and die? Just because I have money? Not all the money in the world is worth one of these men losing his life. I would give anything to have my father back.

Kurt got up and slid back the boxcar door and looked out at the passing scenery. The image of Penelope came to him.

I wonder what she is doing. Is she thinking of me? Does she still love me? Will she still love me after this? All these confused thoughts spun in Kurt's head, and he shook it in frustration and closed the boxcar door.

The train car swayed, rattled, and rumbled and the wheels clicked and clacked. Lulled by the steady motion, Kurt lay down and fell asleep. The others in the boxcar settled down and they, too, rested.

Hours later, Shorty handed out bread and cheese. The group began to gather their gear, and the train slowed and stopped. Shorty slid open the boxcar door, and the men carried everything out. Carlos and Issy opened the other cattle car and pulled down a ramp. They unloaded the horses. Replacing the ramp, the men closed the doors, waved to the engineer; and the train was on its way, clattering into the distance.

Each man saddled and loaded gear onto horses. The saddlebags were heavy with ammunition. Wong Lee, out of his element with handling a Western saddle, tried to help Consuelo and her baby. No one wanted to embarrass the proud little man, so Kurt saddled Consuelo's and the little man's horse. Kurt helped the girl mount, and Wong Lee handed the baby up. The group started their journey toward town.

The men discussed what to do since they would not reach Red Wing until dusk. Kurt said he would send someone for Father Torres. They hoped to learn from the priest the location of Poindexter's men and how many there were. That information would dictate their actions. One thing Kurt wouldn't do was go barging in and get everyone killed.

They arrived near town at dark and stopped in a brush-filled gully. Kurt asked Ramone to put on his old clothes and walk to the church and ask for the priest. He told him to be careful and walk slowly.

They waited out in the brush for what seemed like hours. The men were becoming impatient, and Kurt was growing more anxious as time went on. Then they heard rustling and a dark-robed figure, some Mexicans, and Ramone walked into the gully.

"Ahhh, it is so good to see you, Señor Kurt," greeted the priest. "I see you have brought others with you—and a mother and child. I am so glad that you are safe. We must hurry. We can save introductions for later. You will leave your horses here, and they will be cared for. Follow me. There is a shorter route to the cellar of the church."

Father Torres led them up the gully. They came closer to town and then walked toward some animal sheds and a small stable built of adobe. They entered. Inside there were horses. The place smelled of manure and hay. Father Torres went to a wall on which hung a saddle and ropes. He pushed on a board and the wall moved. A hidden door opened. The priest took a lantern from a nail on the wall, lit it, and walked carefully down very narrow steps. The others followed. It was necessary to hold hands as the lantern light became obstructed by those walking ahead. They were in a cave, and instinctively they lowered their heads and proceeded. What little light there was remained dim in the damp stale air of the cavern. Cobwebs touched their faces. In a few moments they turned a corner and there was more light. They walked towards the light and went through a door into a large room located directly beneath the church sanctuary.

"You are full of surprises, Father," said Shorty. "Were you expecting trouble?"

The priest smiled. "It is very mysterious and intriguing, is it not? The tunnel, we did not build. It was dug many years ago by our ancestors. We simply built on top of it. Now we put it to good use."

"Father Torres," asked Kurt. "What is going on above us?"

"Señor Kurt, I have much news—very detailed and helpful—but first you must introduce me to your friends. Ramone, I have, of course, met."

"Well, Father, this is Consuelo and her baby. Consuelo is Ramone's sister."

Father Torres walked over and greeted the young woman, then placed his hand on the baby, as if in blessing.

"This is Griz, another plainsman like Jedidiah. And that is Wong Lee, a master of fighting skills. He is from China. And this is Bill Banks, and the others are Tom Williams, Spider, Jack, Sam, and Buster. They have agreed to fight for Wet Springs."

Father Torres shook the hand of each man as he was introduced, then turned to Kurt, "Very well done. Kurt, I regret to say, in your absence much has happened. Let me start with your mother. I must tell you she has been very ill and we are not sure of her recovery."

"Is the doctor with her?" asked Kurt.

"No, he did all he could for her, and now she is being cared for by Mrs. Bennett. The rest of your crew is guarding the ranch.

I am sorry to say it appears that Jedidiah went off on

his own to ambush Poindexter's Ranch. For three days he fired upon Poindexter's buildings and men. We believe he is no longer alive. It is said he took his killers with him, and that he still lies unburied. And your father," the priest stopped and put his hand on Kurt's shoulder, knowing the boy's grief was still fresh, "we buried him with a small ceremony up near the canyon at the face of a cliff. We hope to have a memorial service in his honor when your mother is better and this terrible fighting is over."

"Thank you, Father," said Kurt struggling to control his emotions.

"Now, as to the town and the number and location of Poindexter's men, I have information." Father Torres produced a piece of paper from his robes.

"Poindexter's men have been in town for several days now and are stationed in specific places. My people have been spying, and as news comes to me, I write it down. Together they counted maybe fifty men waiting in ambush. Some are on the roofs, some in buildings, and others at barricades on both ends of the street. We don't know exactly how many men there are. But, we do know they eat, sleep, and hardly move from their positions. Worse, we don't know which side some of the merchants are on."

"We can't fight that many," said Kurt. "Perhaps we should go back to the ranch and…"

"A few days before I would have told you it was hopeless," said Father Torres, "but let me tell you, Dr. Bennett and I, God forgive me, have organized a vigilante committee. We will let your men take the brunt of the fighting on Main Street, and we will fight those in the stores. Not everyone in town is with Poindexter."

"How many on our side, Father?" asked Kurt.

"Perhaps enough," said Father Torres. "Maybe more will join in if we do well. As I said, Dr. Bennett and I will attack the stores on both sides of Main Street. And you can split your group and attack the men on the street and those on the roofs.

"What else do you suggest?" asked Kurt.

"The men on the roofs are the big problem. If you could figure a way to subdue the shooters up there, I believe we would be a long way towards winning this fight."

Kurt and Shorty discussed it among themselves. Who could slip silently onto the roofs and disable these men? The answer was obvious—Wong Lee. How many could he take out before they saw and killed him? If the little man was willing, it was a risk they had to take.

Father Torres brought food and drink to the cellar. They ate the late supper in tense silence. Kurt asked the priest about his cat and was told he was recovering. Cindy was with the other horses and away from the fighting.

"What bothers me the most," said Kurt, "is that we are asking men to risk their lives for us."

"Ah, but Señor Kurt," replied the priest, "didn't you tell them that when you hired them? And, did you not tell them that their reward would be lifetime employment? Is not that your reputation? Tonight we plan; tomorrow, we act. We shall remove the undesirables. Yes, we risk our lives, but it is time this evil stops."

Kurt looked at Shorty, Carlos, and Issy, then at his newly hired men.

"Alright," he said. "Wong Lee, will you climb the roof and eliminate the men with rifles? We don't know how many are up there, maybe a lot."

"It is an honor to fight against these bad men. Wong Lee will not die. I have much reason to live." He looked toward Consuelo and the baby.

"Looky here," said Griz. "You bought me this big Sharps, and I have three hundred rounds of ammunition. I could climb the bell tower and protect Lee. Should Wong Lee get into trouble, I'll cover him."

"The noise of that blasted .50 caliber will wake every bad man in town," argued Shorty.

"At some point," said the priest, "the element of surprise will be lost. Señor Griz, the tower has a chair I put up there myself. You are right; you can look down on all the rooftops of town."

"We must agree," said Kurt, "that no one can begin the fight until the men on the roof are taken care of. Griz, you'll need a signal of some kind, maybe a brightly colored scarf with a rock in it, to throw down as a sign to attack?"

"We have to confront the men from inside the barriers at the same time," said Shorty. "I suggest that after we see Griz's signal, we split up and attack each barricade. Once we begin fighting, Father Torres' people can join in. What do you think, Father?"

"I think we can do no better, Señores. After I pray, I will go and tell Dr. Bennett so he can alert his people to be ready for tomorrow morning."

It was getting late. It was unlikely, however, that anyone would get much sleep. The priest said goodnight, saying something about going to the church.

Before dawn, Shorty awakened Kurt and the rest of the Wet Springs crew. Kurt, Spider, Jack, Sam, Buster, and Ramone started for the west barricade. Griz climbed up to his post in the tower with the big Sharps and a Winchester .44. Wong Lee was dressed in black and had on soft-soled shoes. He carried the bow in his hand and a quiver over his back. On his chest, he had buckled the leather band that held the knives. Shorty, Tom, Bill, Carlos, and Issy headed for the east barricade.

The men moved quietly down the stone steps and met the first faint light of the morning sky. For once it was cloudy, very dark, and looked like rain. Father Torres was outside the church watching. Hiding behind the open doors of the church, were a number of men armed with old guns, clubs, and hatchets waiting in anticipation of the signal.

This was a great number of people to move silently. The plan was to proceed in ones and twos and pretend they were about normal business. It was hoped that the guards would be too bored or indifferent to interfere.

The first to move was Wong Lee. Then the others by ones and twos filtered through town. Griz continued to watch from the bell tower.

In the shadows of the roofs, Wong Lee's clothes would make him nearly invisible. This was a problem for Griz but an advantage against the gunman. Wong Lee ran silently, wrapped his legs around a post, pushed his body higher, and effortlessly pulled himself onto the roof. He took the bow from around his shoulders and nocked an arrow. Silently he moved up higher and looked out over the other roofs of the small town.

Many of the guards weren't doing a very good job. Wong Lee could see only two men standing. He couldn't make out where the other guards were. Perhaps they were lying down, or even asleep. How was he to find them and put each one out of commission, if he couldn't see them? He would have to think of something fast.

Wong Lee walked forward very slowly until he saw a dark lump. He wasn't sure whether it was a man or not. He made a bird call. The lump moved and sat up. Wong Lee let fly his arrow and it struck with a "fump." He walked over, and the man was reaching for his rifle. The arrow was stuck dead center and almost went through his body. The man spit up blood and then fell over dead.

This is how it went for Wong Lee on the roofs of buildings all along the north side of Main Street. He eliminated eight men in less than twelve minutes; not one of them had heard him coming or had a chance to warn the others. Silently, the wiry little man climbed down off a lower roof and slid down a post. He crossed the street and shinnied up another and onto a roof. By the same method, he continued to eliminate Poindexter's men.

Abruptly, he came upon a group of three. At the same time, they saw Wong Lee and bent down to get their rifles. They were slow, and he shot the man in the middle with an arrow. Then he threw a knife and killed the second man. But the third raised his rifle and shot. Wong Lee was struck by the bullet and fell.

The third man was levering another shell for a second shot when the terrific boom of the Sharps echoed through the town. Poindexter's man fell.

There were still four men left on the roofs on the south side of Main Street. Griz reloaded, and when the first of the four popped up, he shot and killed him. Griz reloaded again and shot a second man. The two remaining guards, seeing that someone from the bell tower was picking them off, remained hidden. It was still early dawn, and roof shadows provided deep cover.

Griz waited. The vigilante committee stood at their assigned positions. Poindexter's men at both barricades were up and alert, as well as those hiding in the stores. The sky slowly began to lighten.

Griz finally spotted the third man. "Boom," went the big .50 caliber. The plainsman did not miss. The last remaining rifleman shot at Griz and hit the big bell behind him. Bong! Griz removed his hands from his ears and searched through the scope for that last flash of fire. When it went off again, Griz shot at the flash. Again the outlaw's bullet hit the bell, and it rang. So did Griz's ears. The only thing he could hear now was a deafening buzz.

Griz looked through his scope and couldn't be certain what his last shot had done. The sun rose, and he could see the man was lying dead on the roof. The plainsman reached for the crimson scarf and threw it up high into the air. It could be clearly seen by those below.

Kurt on the west side, and Shorty and his crew on the east side, waited impatiently. They finally saw the fluttering arc of the scarf. Instantly the air exploded in gunfire, as the Wet Springs crew fired from the edge of buildings into the gunslingers' barricades. Some lived to turn and fire, but with no cover, they had little chance. Many died where they stood.

Shots rang out from various buildings on both sides of the street as more of Poindexter's men fired at Kurt and Shorty's crew. Kurt took a bullet in the leg and went down. Similarly, Ramone, Carlos, Spider, and Bill were quickly wounded. Buster came out into the street, revealing himself, and let fly with his double-barreled, sawed-off shotguns. He hit at least two men and put the fear of God into the others.

Then a strange growling noise from the angry mob began softly. It quickly grew loud and menacing. One of Poindexter's men ran out into the street from the dry goods store. He put his hands in the air and yelled, "I give up! I give up! Don't shoot!"

A crowd of Mexican men with clubs, hand scythes, and axes ran at him, and he quickly died from the many blows.

"It is too late to surrender," yelled one of the vigilantes.

If there were any more outlaws left, they either ran or escaped in some manner undetected by the mob. Otherwise, any living Poindexter man found was summarily executed by these enraged citizens.

Dr. Bennett leading one group of men, and Father Torres leading another group of equally serious vigilantes, joined forces in the middle of the street.

"Father Torres," said Bennett. "You have your list, and I have mine. We wake up these people, and they have two or three hours before the train comes, to sell their businesses and leave. Let's roust them out and bring them back here."

Within a half-hour, some very indignant citizens,

some still in their nightclothes, stood in the middle of the street. This included men, women, and children. Among the group were Reverend Pellett and his wife, the banker and his wife, the judge, and his wife, and many of the merchants who refused trade or who charged double for their goods. Mr. Schmidt, the restaurant owner, was there, some Mexican businessmen who catered to Poindexter, and many more gamblers, bartenders, women, and clerks.

The vigilante's simmering hatred over their twenty-year oppression by Poindexter now boiled over. They were not to be trifled with. The message was, be on the train or die. Poindexter's associates could take what they could carry, and whatever was left would be sold or given away. The banker was supervised by the town's trusted bank clerk to see that the scoundrel didn't take one penny more than he was entitled to. Basically, most of Poindexter puppets were going to leave town with only the clothes on their backs.

"It's not fair," shouted Reverend Pellett. "You people can't take the law into your own hands. At least extend a Christian attitude!"

"Like you did, preacher?" Shouted Dr. Bennett. "I'll tell you what's not fair about this, Reverend. That you, a man of God, consorted with a man who oppressed an entire town and territory with gunmen and thugs. He killed, he stole, he rustled cattle, he beat and harassed citizens, and set himself up as a demi-god. And you, Reverend, you helped him. You sanctioned his actions, you honored him, you accepted his dirty money. We of this citizens vigilante committee find you guilty. Any of you who stay, or return, will be tarred and feathered or hanged. Do you have anything else to say, Pellett?"

There was no answer, only a look of fear and resignation on the faces of those marked to leave town.

Three very official-looking men rode into the midst of this scene. They looked at the vigilante committee, the street littered with dead men, and they sat stock-still on their horses. Townspeople armed with clubs, hoes, and guns moved menacingly closer to the three newcomers.

"Whoa!" said one of the three men, holding a badge and his hands up defensively. "Two territorial deputies and one US Marshall here. Now, you folks take it easy."

The doctor, even more furious, came forward. "I'm Dr. Bennett, and for several years now I've been writing—pleading—for help from you folks. You never even answered me. Now that we've taken care of it ourselves and we're nearly finished, you ride into town? Your help is not wanted. Get out, or we'll take care of you too, for dereliction of duty."

The crowd, really heated now, yelled in loud fervor and, having already killed a number of Poindexter's gunmen, were ready to continue without inhibition. The three lawmen on horseback knew their fate rested on their diplomatic skills. Never in their careers had they encountered anything like this. Someone better think fast.

"Wait a minute! Where's your sheriff?"

"He skipped town, the coward!" yelled someone from the crowd. "He was more crooked than most. He's yet to be found and dealt with."

"The territorial governor gave us papers authorizing us to

appoint someone sheriff until you have new elections," said the governor's appointee. "Is Kurt West or Shorty here?"

Kurt limped forward and Shorty walked over, noting for the first time that Kurt was wounded.

"Here's the papers. Here's the badges." said one of the lawmen. "Shorty, raise your right hand. What's your last name?"

"If you have to know, Jones," said Shorty.

"Under the authorization of the territorial governor, Shorty Jones, I hereby appoint you sheriff, Kurt West is your deputy. Now everything you do will be legal. Once you have this sorted out, come and report to us. We'll check into the hotel over there, and stay out of your way."

"Well, at least you've done something right. Anything more or less, and you would have been in trouble," yelled Dr. Bennett.

The crowd roared their agreement.

Griz had climbed up on the roof where he last saw Wong Lee. What a man that little Chinese was! He had moves Griz had never seen before, not even from Sioux Indians. He counted dead bodies, as he moved forward across the roofs. Then he saw Wong Lee in his black outfit. How small and frail he looked. Griz turned the young man gently over, and Wong Lee groaned. There was a gaping hole in his side, and blood was oozing out. Griz plugged the hole and ripped off his belt and tied it around the skinny man to hold down the kerchief.

Griz bellowed, "Get the doctor up here! And I mean now! If he don't come quick thars going to be trouble!"

Griz held his Sharps .50 in the air and shot it. Boom!

"Get a doctor up here now; Wong Lee's alive, but he's hurt bad!"

"Coming, Griz," yelled Shorty. "We're coming."

Dr. Bennett, holding his medical bag, climbed up a ladder onto the roof and examined Wong Lee's wound. He immediately thought there was no way this man could survive. There was too much blood loss. Nevertheless, Bennett assembled what he needed. He followed the path of the bullet. The wound was an ugly lacerated mess, but no vital organs were hit. With great care, he washed the wounds with carbolic acid and eased the bullet out and sewed Wong Lee together.

"It's best we don't move him," said the doc. "Griz, will you stay up here and build a shelter? He needs to stay hydrated."

"Doc?" asked Griz.

"It means to keep his lips moist and try to give him water. I'll check on him every day. If he wakes, come and get me."

Griz went below, gathered some things from stores—without paying—went back on the roof and made a makeshift tent. The plainsman would remain and look out for this brave little man.

Dr. Bennett examined Kurt, Carlos, and the others and treated and bandaged their wounds. Bill had the worst of it and was bedridden. He lost a finger, and was shot in the shoulder and the leg. Bill's pard, Tom, would look after him.

The vigilante committee met in Pellett's church after they forced those on the list to leave on the train. Kurt and

Shorty were there and listened. Tempers flared, and there was shouting and talk of burning Poindexter's home. Kurt finally stood up and stated that Mrs. Cynthia Poindexter and her daughter, Penelope Hathaway, were innocent victims. The crowd got ugly with this. They shouted out that no one was innocent living with that man.

"I saw Poindexter and that Penelope in a carriage the other day headed for the big house. Don't tell me she's innocent."

"Penelope? Home?" thought Kurt.

His heart leaped. But to hear her accused in this way turned him cold. Kurt looked at the man and touched his pistol.

"Be prepared to back up that statement with a gun, mister, or don't be here when I get back."

Kurt limped to the stable. He found a mustang in a stall, grabbed a bridle, and threw it on. He did the same with the first saddle he could find. He jumped on the horse's back and was on his way to Poindexter's ranch. Nothing mattered except to see Penelope and to protect her. There was no telling what Poindexter would do to her now that his empire had fallen—especially if any word got back to him about her involvement with Kurt.

Shorty watched Kurt run to the stable, but he couldn't keep up. Seeing the horseflesh he rode away on, Shorty knew he'd never stay with him. The older man picked out the best looking mount left in the corral, saddled, and rode after his boss.

Gradually Kurt began to see that he would kill the horse if he didn't ease off. The mount was missing gait and coughing for air. Flecks of foam flew off the withers and neck of the horse and onto his pants. Kurt slowed to a walk, and the animal began to recover.

It was late afternoon when Kurt arrived at the mansion. It was eerily quiet. There was no movement, no sound. It looked abandoned. Kurt rode up to the front door and got down. The horse hung its head, totally exhausted. Kurt opened one of the double front doors and went inside. He was amazed at the place. How huge! How ornate with tiled floors and stained glass. The wounded young man limped into the great room and noted its enormous chandelier, the wide curving staircase, the richly patterned rugs, and then he stopped. Poindexter's twisted body lay in a pool of blood at the bottom of the stairs.

Kurt heard a noise coming from a room to the right, and a man walked out chewing on a chicken leg. It was Sheriff Engler. The sheriff dropped the meat, stared at the star on Kurt's chest. A deep growl emanated from the older man's throat.

"So Poindexter is dead, I see," said Kurt.

"I didn't do it," snarled Engler. "I found him that way! I don't know who did it. I came here for help and..."

Engler realized who he was talking to and stopped. His eyes narrowed

"Where are your big, brave deputies now, Engler?" asked Kurt.

"They deserted me, the cowards. I did what you said, I got out of town. Looks like you won. So I guess I'll be headin' out."

"I don't think so. What I said was if I saw you again, I

would shoot you on sight. Now draw!"

"No," he whimpered, his steely stare belying his nervous facade.

Kurt drew his pistol and shot Engler, barely skimming the right shin. Engler yelled and staggered but did not fall.

"Now draw!"

"No!" he pleaded.

Kurt watched the muscle tense on Engler's right hand.

"Now draw, or I'll whittle you to pieces."

Without warning, Engler reached, and it was a lightning draw. His gun went off, and the bullet nicked Kurt's side. The newly appointed lawman drew and shot, and the bullet struck the other man's belt buckle. Engler fired again. It took a slice of skin from Kurt's left arm. Taking no chances, Kurt emptied his six-shooter into this devious man. Engler fell back and died.

Kurt bound up his wounds as best he could and then with great trepidation began to search the mansion— looking for Penelope. He didn't find her. Kurt could no longer stand the smell of the place. It was the stench of death and oppression. It fitted that mangy character. Kurt walked outside and saw Shorty riding toward him. The older man started to speak, and Kurt held up his hand. Shorty shrugged and went into the house to look for himself. He came back and sat down on the stone steps.

"Want to tell me about it?"

"Not right now, Shorty. Later."

"Kurt, you don't know if she's dead or hurt. She's not in the house. Where would she go for help? To your place, maybe? Let's try there."

With renewed hope, Kurt painfully mounted his tired horse, and they headed for Wet Springs. They came upon a circle of boulders, and a flock of buzzards flew up. Shorty got off his horse and climbed the hill of stone. He gagged and held his nose. The stench was overwhelming.

"Three bodies, Kurt," Shorty called out. "Looks like two dead Indians and old man Jedidiah. The buzzards haven't reached him. You stay put, I'll bury him."

Shorty dragged what was left of the Indians out onto the flats. It wasn't long, and the buzzards were on them. Kurt watched as his older partner rode back to the house and returned with a blanket and shovel. His friend dug a hole, wrapped Jedidiah's body, and lowered it into the grave. Dirt was shoveled over him along with a covering of rocks.

"That was one brave old man," said Shorty. "Soon as we can, we'll make this right."

They got back on their horses and headed home. Kurt was shot in three places, and all of them hurt like the devil. He was exhausted and sickened by the events of this endless day. Yet, it was still not over. He had to find Penelope.

"Why so gloomy?" asked Shorty. "You should be grateful this thing is finally finished."

Just then the sky flashed with light, and there was a huge crackling boom. Lightning and thunder—then came the rain in a terrific downpour. By the time Kurt and Shorty got their slickers out, they were soaked.

Did that loudmouth in town know what he was talking about? Was Penelope really back from the East? This thought was what kept Kurt going through the endless miles.

The horses began to slip and slide in the mud. The men rode for several hours, traveling steadily up to the high country of Wet Springs. Sticky adobe clay stuck to the horses' hooves and legs. It seemed to take forever to reach the ranch house. They were wet, cold, exhausted, and thoroughly hungry. Kurt especially dreaded learning what had become of his mother.

To be on the safe side, they hollered at the house. Mrs. Bennett came running out all smiles. "Thank God you're home. Everything's fine, Kurt. Really. Come in, we have a surprise for you."

Kurt and Shorty wearily dismounted and the older man took the horses to the corral. Kurt limped, dripping wet, into the house. There was a shrill scream and before him stood a beautiful woman wearing a pale blue dress. She ran to Kurt and hugged him. Kurt groaned from his wounds. The woman pulled her hands back, and she had blood on them.

"Oh, he's wounded!" cried Penelope. "Quick, Mrs. West, help me!"

Priscilla was physically changed from her recent illness and recovery. Her eyes were now deep-set and sunken into her cheekbones. Her hair was streaked white. She moved slowly as if she could only do so much in a given moment. The old Priscilla who took charge in a crisis was gone. The tragedy she had endured had left her incapable of great surprise or emotion. She was a survivor, but a badly wounded one.

Kurt's eyes misted, but he smiled tenderly at his mother, stifling his shock at her abrupt change.

"Well, Kurt," said Priscilla, her words soft and low, "I'm still alive and hope to be around to see my grandchildren." Her eyes glimmered slightly, a ray of the old Priscilla shown through. "Now, will you please kiss this girl. She's been yapping about you for the last few hours. After that," continued Priscilla, sounding more like her old self, "take your shirt off and let me see those wounds, and then we'll get to the leg."

Kurt stared at Penelope. "Could this beautiful woman be the girl he had loved so long ago?"

"I imagined a hundred different reunions, but not one like this," said Penelope. "Can't you say anything?"

"Hello," was all that he could manage.

The room filled with laughter. Kurt didn't see anything funny about it.

"Alright, if that's the way you're going to be," said Penelope.

She came forward and kissed him right on the lips in front of everyone. The people in the room whooped. There were Zachary, Rosa, Carmen, Cynthia, Juan, Mrs. Bennett, his mother, and Shorty.

This was too overwhelming for Kurt. He felt very dizzy and that was all he remembered on the way to the floor, except for the sound of a very loud scream.

As Kurt woke up, he recognized his bedroom. He was completely naked between crisp sheets. He had been bathed and his wounds were dressed. He blushed at the thought that his mother or maybe even Penelope would have helped wash him.

Over the next few days and weeks, the story of the shoot-out in town and Kurt's killing of the sheriff was gradually revealed. Poindexter's death remained a mystery. Kurt neither confirmed nor denied that he did it. The dramatic events that had occurred in the mansion were known only to Priscilla, Kurt, Penelope, and Cynthia.

CHAPTER THIRTY-THREE

Cynthia, not able to endure any association with her dead husband, refused to be called Poindexter and changed her name back to Hathaway. As the weeks passed, she grew stronger and gained weight, thanks to the cooking of Rosa and Carmen. Penelope's mother was like Priscilla in many ways. Both had aged in a short period of time. Both were newly widowed and survivors of deeply shocking ordeals. They were both terribly damaged by life, yet still willing to confront it in their own fragile ways.

Cynthia and Priscilla were inseparable. One afternoon as the ladies were sitting on the great porch overlooking Wet Springs, Mrs. West reached over to take her friend's hand.

"Cynthia, you have become dearer to me than a sister. Neither of us is getting any younger. Our children love each other, and I would be surprised if they did not marry soon. Stay here with me, make Wet Springs your home."

"Priscilla, you cannot imagine what this offer means to me. I have been terrified of returning to that horrible place. If you are truly certain you don't mind if I live here, I can't think of any other home I would rather have."

Priscilla was on her feet, hugging her friend. Both were crying.

Cynthia Hathaway asked Kurt to handle her affairs.

Kurt arrived at the mansion by wagon and found that someone had dragged the bodies of Sheriff Engler and Poindexter outdoors. After the vultures, coyotes, and other vermin had their fill, all that was left were parts of the skull, jawbones, and teeth-scarred rib cages. Kurt felt only grim satisfaction that these men could no longer cause pain to anyone he loved.

Kurt gathered two safes—one at the big house and another from Poindexter's saloon. Once at Wet Springs, Cynthia asked for a blacksmith to come from town. He opened both safes. She discovered thirty thousand dollars, deeds, and many legal papers. What was inside both safes would take years to go through and dispose.

Cynthia's intention was to find the previous owners Poindexter had cheated. She wanted to right the wrongs to whatever extent possible. Even when this task was accomplished, the holdings from her first husband's business would leave Cynthia and Penelope very wealthy indeed.

Father Torres came to the ranch and inquired when they would like to have the memorial services for Señor West and Jedidiah. He brought stonecutters with him, and they went to both gravesites and carved epitaphs on the stones over their graves. John's was simple:

Here lies John West, beloved husband and father.
He was an honest and courageous man.

We shall miss him.

Jedidiah's epitaph was chiseled on the bare rock where he was buried:

Here lies a hero.

He never shirked his duty.

He died so others could live.

Mountain man, hunter, fighter extraordinaire.

Father Torres said both the white and Mexican sides of the town agreed to work together to ensure safety and peace. After much discussion, they had voted Zachary to be the new sheriff and Ramone his deputy—two reformed men to keep the law and maintain order.

It was Shorty who had ridden back and filled the territorial lawmen and U.S. Marshal in on the details of the fight.

"Can't say things were handled exactly to the law," one deputy said, "but I don't think we'll be needed around here." The lawmen wrote names and dates in their reports and left town.

The day of the church memorial services, people came from miles around to pay tribute to their friend and neighbor, John West, and to the mountain man they had come to admire and respect. As the last prayer was said, the mourners spilled out onto the street for the largest wake the town had ever held. It became a celebration of hope for the future.

Kurt, along with Shorty, left the party early. They visited Wong Lee at Dr. Bennett's office with its small hospital. They had finally managed to get the brave little man off the roof. When they walked into the hospital room, old Griz was right beside his new friend. There, too, was Consuelo holding the young man's hand and smiling modestly.

"I told you, boss, Wong Lee not die. When do you give me land? Consuelo, baby, and I need place to live and raise children."

It was the first time Kurt and Shorty laughed out loud since the fight ended.

"Just as soon as you get out of that bed, Wong Lee. But I insist you get married first."

"Wong Lee already married, Boss. We did that this morning."

Shorty and Kurt smiled in great surprise. Shorty joined his boss and echoed his best wishes.

CHAPTER THIRTY-FOUR

Returning to Wet Springs, Kurt locked little Tiger in his room with food and water. Cindy was staying in the corral with the other horses. Kurt was walking today. A rarity, but he had time to spare, and he needed to think.

Shorty was seeing that Mexican gal again. Issy was going to marry Maria. Griz was somehow tied to Wong Lee, and they were the best of friends. Bill was recovering from his wounds and would make an excellent ranch hand. The same could be said for Tom, Spider, Jack, Sam, and Buster. Ramone and Zachary were off being lawmen.

So, thought Kurt as he absentmindedly kicked a rock ahead of him as he walked, *where does that leave me? I have the ranch and a great crew. There are still the cattle and horses that take my time. Mother has changed and has no interest in the ranch now. How strange! She does take great comfort in her friends, though. She loves Cynthia, Carmen, and Rosa. Anyone can see that.*

Kurt made it to the cliff and began to climb the base to Promontory Point. It was hot, and he took his time. As he climbed, beads of sweat appeared on his brow. He took the narrow foot trail and in a few minutes came out on top. As always, it was a glorious view. From behind, Kurt heard a noise.

"Kurt West, I've been waiting for you every day. You made me a promise. Remember?"

"That was just kid's stuff, Penelope."

She lashed out in anger and pushed Kurt. "You! Won't you ever learn how to talk to a woman? Kid stuff? Back East, those rich boys tried to paw me. All I could think about was you. Apologize!"

"I'm sorry. I didn't mean to hurt..."

"Now come closer."

He did as she asked. This strange, beautiful woman put her arms around him.

"Now tell me how much you love me, and do it right."

"Every day you were gone, Penelope, I thought about you."

"Yes?"

"Every day I yearned for one of your letters. I even dreamed about you. Each day I wondered if you really loved me."

"Yes, Kurt, yes. Is that all?"

"At fourteen you were beautiful, but now..."

"Yes?"

"Perfection. I'm afraid you've...stolen my heart."

"Would you like to kiss me, Kurt?"

He nodded his head.

"Then what's stopping you?"

"Pure fear," he said, not smiling.

"The great Kid Kurt is afraid of me?"

"Yes."

Penelope took Kurt's hand and led him to their ledge on the rock. She sat and pulled him down beside her.

"Do you remember that first time we sat here?" Penelope whispered, and she reached up and put her arms around his neck. She pulled his head down until his lips met hers.

"Yes," he gasped as he felt her supple body against his chest. He answered her kiss for kiss.

Blissful moments passed as this young man gave his heart over to this lovely girl.

Eventually, they found a comfortable position and looked out over Wet Springs Ranch. The buildings far below took on a magical appearance from this great height. The day was serene and lovely. The sky was clear, and a light summer breeze blew and cooled the hot, dry air. These two young lovers enjoyed the moment and each other.

"Mother has given me the ranch, cattle, and horses. How am I ever going to manage them?" Penelope asked.

"Seems to me you need a foreman and a lot of loyal cowhands."

"Would you agree to take over for me, Kurt?"

"Only if you'll marry me and continue to live on Wet Springs," grinned the young man.

"All right, Mr. Kurt West. You drive a hard bargain, but I think I can agree to do that."

She kissed him. The kiss was long and sweet and held promises for tomorrow. Vibrant pink and red hues of sunset cast shadows across the valley as the lovers, holding each other's hands, started their descent, confident that united they would be worthy guardians of WET SPRINGS RANCH.

**Kurt and Penelope look over
Wet Springs Ranch.**

Dear Reader,

If you enjoyed reading FIGHT FOR WET SPRINGS, please help promote the book by posting a review on Amazon.com and following Charlie Steel on social media.

https://www.facebook.com/CharlieSteelAuthor
https://www.goodreads.com/author/show/3484434.
Charlie_Steel

Charlie Steel may also be contacted at cowboytails@ juno.com or by writing to the following address:

Charlie Steel
c/o Condor Publishing, Inc.
PO Box 39
Lincoln, Michigan 48742

Warm greetings from Condor Publishing, Inc.
Gail Heath, publisher